A Clean Bill Of Health

Patsy Collins

Contents

1. Accidents Happen

There was no way to avoid hitting the car which roared out the side road. I braked hard and awoke in hospital.

I looked at my arm, already plastered. "Can I go?"

"Not yet. You were unconscious so we're keeping an eye on you."

I wasn't seeing double and knew who I was: Serena Jones, teacher, sixty-three, single. That last is my choice, not Mum's. She'd have liked to see me married but in that, like many other things, I've been a disappointment.

I wasn't planned. Mum was going to university, but married Dad instead when they discovered I was on the way. Carrie was planned.

"I wanted another girl as a friend for you," Mum said.

I know they loved me, but I've always felt a little guilty. Without me, Mum would have had a career. Dad wouldn't have had to work so hard. Did I make amends by being the perfect daughter? Of course not.

Fortunately my rebellious antics didn't lead Carrie astray. Her hair stayed the soft chestnut she'd inherited from Mum. Her clothes were school uniform or pretty dresses. My sister worked hard at school, got a good job and good husband. She still has them, plus a lovely house and two lovely children, who are now providing her with delightful grandchildren. I hope I'm not sounding cynical. I'm happy for Carrie and rather wish I were like her, but I'm not.

As soon as I could leave school I was off travelling.

I went wherever I could afford to get to and did anything I could to pay my way to the next destination. Years passed. I visited Kathmandu, Timbuktu and the Yucatan. I danced at Glastonbury, climbed up Uluru and down into Petra. I swam with dolphins, rode camels and fed orphan elephants. The view from my tent, hut or room was of a volcanic crater, mighty ocean, or dry river bed. I picked fruit, waitressed and packed boxes. I even panned for gold. Somehow I never made it to Amsterdam but otherwise there wasn't a hippie hotspot I didn't see.

I took gap years from my travels to get an education. Now I live on a house boat, perhaps to compensate for never taking a cruise or sailing trip, and I teach geography. The school overlooks Mum's garden, so I was close by when Mum needed me in the first few months of her widowhood. Carrie didn't neglect her, not at all, but it was easier for me. I felt I'd almost atoned for the disappointments I'd caused her. The holiday was to be part of that. We'd packed everything we might need and set off in plenty of time. Then I'd crashed the car.

Story of my life. It wasn't my fault I'd been conceived, but it messed up Mum's life. Now another accident involving me had stopped her taking the holiday she'd been looking forward to. Or was it worse than that? She'd been right next to me in the car.

"Mum!"

A nurse heard my call. My blood pressure was checked again, I answered questions as a light was shone into my eyes. "You seem fine. The doctor should be round soon and I'm sure he'll discharge you."

"And Mum?"

"I see her coming now."

Mum wasn't wheeled in from theatre as I'd feared but walking on her own two feet.

"I'm so sorry," I whispered.

"It's OK, love. I knew you'd be fine. Remember when you fell out that tree? You couldn't remember your own name for a while but were right as rain by the time the grazes dried. I never have to worry about you, despite how things might look to outsiders."

I started to say that's not what I'd meant, but tears stopped the words. Mum loves me and no accident would ever stop that. It's not the kind of thing I can talk about, so I just allowed her to brush my hair off my face.

"Carrie's coming," Mum said.

My sister timed it perfectly, arriving just as the doctor said I was fit to leave. She provided the paperwork for a holiday insurance claim.

"We can use the money for another trip, Mum," I said.

"I'm afraid not."

"Oh." Although it was understandable she wouldn't want to travel with me anywhere else I couldn't help being hurt.

"I've already spent it. Once I knew you were going to be OK I called the travel agent and explained. She's booking something else."

"The hotel is full the rest of the season."

"We're not going there." She showed us the tickets.

Mum had booked my perfect trip. I couldn't say anything.

Neither could Carrie, but she recovered first. "You've just booked a river cruise in Amsterdam on the spur of the moment?"

Of course she had. She's my mum, isn't she?

2. Owl Overload

Emelie stared at the doorbell of her sister's flat. Below it, where 'Sia Westrom' had once been scrawled in faded biro, was a new piece of neatly lettered card. In place of the tired, white plastic surround to the button was a cute ceramic bird. That seemed like an improvement and it would have been if the bird wasn't an owl. Emilie shouldn't have been surprised. There were so many of the feathered creatures inside the flat they were bound to spill out eventually.

As Emelie stood on the owl-shaped doormat she couldn't help thinking this was all her fault. If she hadn't salvaged that old painting to cheer her sister up six month's ago, maybe Sia could have pulled herself out of her misery without developing this weird and inexplicable owl fixation. Perhaps if she'd not done so much for her sister when she'd first had problems Sia would have been forced to cope with things herself and worked through her unhappiness. Was Emelie a bad sister? Should she learn to mind her own business?

Emelie's doubts about interfering again in her sister's life vanished the moment she pressed the doorbell. No musical chime sounded – instead Emelie heard a hooting call. "This has definitely gone too far!" she said to herself as she waited for Sia to answer. That at least was an improvement. Not so long ago she'd had to keep ringing and ringing until the noise forced Sia to combat her lethargy and open up.

"If you can't leave me alone, why don't you just let yourself in?" she grumbled.

"Because I'm trying to help you, not do everything for you." She wouldn't hesitate to use her own key in an emergency, but not just walking straight in as though it were her own home was a small step towards helping Sia get back her independence and then hopefully some confidence.

"I'm fine now. I don't need help."

Sia did look much better physically and she'd taken the trouble to soften her words with a smile, but… The coat hook on which Emelie hung her jacket was in the form of an owl with talons outstretched to hold items of clothing. Next to it was a matching owl key hook.

"You're over the glandular fever, but you're not OK."

Sia's illness had come shortly after she'd broken up with her boyfriend and then lost her temporary job as a hotel receptionist. For a time Emelie did almost everything for her sister – shopping, cooking, and cleaning. Emelie hadn't minded the extra work. Sia was too exhausted to care for herself and what are big sisters for if not to help out when needed? What did bother her was that Sia had left every decision to Emelie, not expressing a preference for items of food, times she visited or even if lights were on or off. "Whatever you like," was her answer to everything.

Gradually the symptoms of her illness eased, but Sia didn't seem to properly regain her interest in life. Although she kept herself clean and tidy she wore only her oldest clothes. No doubt they were comfortable, but they were faded and drab. She hardly left the flat except to go, at night, to the twenty-four hour supermarket because Emelie, hoping it was the right thing to do, insisted Sia try to look after herself. Could her habit of hunkering down in her cosy nest and only going out at night account for her affinity with owls?

Emelie, not knowing how to help had attempted to contact Sia's oldest friend Oliver. He'd always had the knack of making her laugh and encouraging her in everything she did. It was he who'd persuaded Sia that her experience working for his parents in the holidays meant she had a good chance of getting the hotel chambermaid job. Without Oliver she might never have applied and gone on to become a receptionist, something she'd loved doing. Of course then she wouldn't have been made redundant, or met her awful boyfriend, but Oliver wasn't to blame for those things. The two had virtually lost touch because Sia's ex had been the jealous type, but Oliver had sent birthday and Christmas cards, so Emelie had been hopeful he'd be willing to renew the friendship. She'd not told Sia of her plan in case she was unsuccessful and added to her disappointments.

When Emelie had reached the huge house Oliver's parents had run as a B&B, she was glad she'd kept the visit to herself. Nobody answered her knock and the place appeared to have been empty for some time. Seeing it looking so tatty, almost as though someone had started to dismantle it and then left nature to take its course, would have upset Sia. She'd spent so many happy hours there, helping Oliver with his chores in exchange for a little pocket money and more free time for the pair to spend on daft schemes together. They'd once made and 'planted' paper flowers in the garden because his mum said it lacked colour. Another time they'd set up a business covering classmates' schoolbooks with pictures of their favourite celebrities, which they got from any old magazines they could scrounge. Redesigning the school uniform had been one of their projects. Although it wasn't officially adopted, they were allowed to wear the blazers they'd made.

Outside the B&B was a skip, containing old fittings and broken furniture. Emelie recognised the turquoise paint of the patio chairs, as Sia had come home with some of it in her hair after she and Oliver had smartened them up as a surprise for his parents. She'd retained a keen interest in all kinds of arts and crafts until she met her ex. After that, work and trying to keep him happy had left her with no time for her hobbies. Would Sia have been saddened to see the chairs thrown out, or pleased they'd apparently stayed in use until fairly recently?

Emelie had reached her car before she turned back for another look in the skip. Something had registered in her subconscious… That was it, the chipped corner of an ornate picture frame. Emelie reached inside, shifted a few pieces of junk and retrieved what had once been a rather lovely painting. The last time she'd seen it was hanging in the hallway of the house, keeping a welcoming eye on visitors, paying and otherwise. Maybe it would remind Sia of happier times. Emelie had rescued the battered picture and taken it to her sister.

"You used to be good at repairing and restoring things. Why not take it up again, at least until you get another job? I bet this would look great if you put the frame back together and cleaned the glass."

"It needs more than that."

"Such as?"

"The plaster moulding is broken. I'd have to repair that and gild it again. As for the painting itself…" She picked it up and studied it carefully, as though assessing how much work would be involved in putting it right.

"Will you try? For me?"

Sia had reluctantly agreed. Together the sisters looked up information on cleaning old paintings, and ordered what Sia would need to make a start. It had taken more coaxing from Emelie before Sia began the work, but once she did, she kept going. Over time she'd transformed the painting, which of course had been of an owl, and began the same process of repair on herself.

At first Emelie was delighted in the change brought about by the painting, and encouraged Sia to work on something else. She'd liked owls as a child and collected a few things decorated with them, or made into owl-like shapes, so Emelie found her an owl ornament in need of attention. Once she'd made that look perfect, Sia started finding her own owls to restore.

"You're regressing to your childhood, having all these," Emelie teased.

"I sort of am – I've reconnected with Oliver."

"That's great! Does he like owls too?"

"Everyone does, don't they?" Sia asked.

"I suppose they do." Sia's interest went way beyond that, but at the time Emelie didn't want to speak against something which seemed to be helping. She'd made a few more enquiries about Oliver, and Sia's thoughts on getting another job, but the replies were evasive. Emelie told herself it was good that her sister was no longer relying so heavily on her and developing a life of her own.

Sia painted and stitched. She bought damaged ornaments, cleaned and repaired them, carefully finishing the painted decoration until it was often better than the original. She'd even created a few new pieces. Attending evening classes allowed her to learn more restoration techniques, and acquiring new items to work on, and the supplies she needed, got her out in the daytime too. She was on friendly terms with others who shared her now varied range of interests. That all seemed like an improvement. It would have been except every single project she worked on was owl related.

The owls quite literally took over Sia's life. Owl pictures hung on every wall, ornaments and knick-knacks covered every surface. Sia offered tea in mugs decorated with owls, poured from a teapot covered in an owl cosy, accompanied by owl shaped biscuits on an owl plate. The whole lot was arranged on an owl tray. Owls were embroidered on bathroom towels, a knitted owl covered a spare toilet roll, the soap dish was an owl on a nest. Sia had never been one for unnecessary 'stuff' such as tea cosies and toilet roll covers – the whole thing was way out of control and the doorbell, whilst rather nice as an individual item, was the final straw.

"You've got to stop this thing with the owls," Emelie blurted out the moment Sia let her in.

"And good afternoon to you, too."

"Sorry. Hello," Emelie said.

"I thought you'd be pleased about my 'thing with the owls'. It's you who got me started and it's…"

"I know I did. Sorry about that, but how was I to know you'd become obsessed?"

"I'm not obsessed, honestly."

Emelie moved some of the owl cushions which were heaped on the sofa and sat down. "Is that right?"

She saw Sia was making giant *papier-mâché* letters. They weren't owl shaped, but there was an O, W, L and S. "Owls!" Emelie exclaimed.

"Exactly. It's our initials. Oliver Land and Sia Westrom."

"It's serious between you two then? I thought… "

"Yes, it's serious, but we're not romantically involved. You're right that wasn't ever going to happen."

"What then?"

"We're going into business together. Well kind of. I'll work for him with this 'owl thing' as a sideline."

"Go on."

"Oliver has taken over his parents' bed and breakfast business and has been extending it into a boutique hotel called Owls. These letters are to go up in reception, where I'll work. Everything will be decorated with all this owl stuff – and it will all be for sale to those guests who want to take a souvenir or gift back home."

Emelie felt her eyes grow as big as saucers, or those of an owl, as she listened to these plans and marvelled at her sister's positive and sensible attitude. Then she preened herself for the role she'd played in helping Sia escape the claustrophobic nest she's been sheltering in, and spread her wings again.

As if reading her thoughts Sia thanked Emelie for all her help whilst she was ill, and in finding the painting which had prompted her to contact Oliver. "I've made you something, but now I'm not sure if you'll like it."

"If you made it for me, I'm sure I'll love it."

Sia handed her two tiny owls, suspended on delicate silver earrings. They were exquisite. Emelie went into the bathroom, put them on and admired the effect in the owl shaped mirror. As she turned her head the owls seemed to do the same. Somehow they managed to look both comical and elegant. If she dropped hints maybe Sia would create a matching necklace for her birthday.

"Emelie are you OK in there?" Sia called after a few moments. "You're making a funny noise."

"No, I'm not OK. I've caught your affliction."

"I'm so sorry. I tried to do everything I could so you wouldn't catch ..."

"Not the glandular fever, silly. It's worse than that, I've developed owl mania."

3. A Clean Bill Of Health

I sighed and knocked on Mr Thirlwall's door. Until a few weeks ago he'd been a pleasure to work for. Truthfully, there'd never been much work involved. He hired me as a cleaner, but his flat was always spotless. I changed sheets once a week, loosened lids on jars, drank tea and chatted.

I felt guilty taking his money and doing no work. He said it's his money and my time, if it suits us and doesn't hurt anyone else, why worry? So I tried no to.

"That you, Lydia?" he called.

"Yes, Mr Thirlwall."

As he unlocked the door I wondered what it would be this time. You see, he'd got hold of a medical book and keeps thinking he's got another rare disease. I was fed up taking his temperature, checking for rashes and feeling glands. In my handbag, I had a bottle of food colouring. I'd had the idea of putting it on his flannel and telling him he had green monkey fever. I didn't for fear of what the shock might do to him and kept hold of it to remind me to be nice.

"How are you today, Mr Thirlwall?" I asked, with a sense of dread.

"Name's Taff, and I've got palpitations!"

Palpitations were different from his usual 'ailments'. This could well be genuine.

"How long have they been going on?" I asked.

"It's difficult to say. Could have been happening for ages, without me noticing, couldn't it?"

I wasn't sure about that, but nodded.

He asked me to make tea. Whilst we drank it, he read his medical book. "Says it can be as a result of serious cardiac disease."

"Are there other causes?" Once he has the book open he likes to make use of it.

"It can be anxiety, reaction to drugs, Lown Ganong Levine syndrome …"

"Are you anxious?" I interrupted.

"Well of course I am; I've got unexplained heart palpitations!"

I saw his point and guessed the palpitations would only get worse if he didn't discover the cause.

"Perhaps you should see your doctor?" I suggested.

"I've got an appointment tomorrow."

"Good. He'll soon get to the bottom of this."

"I'm sure you're right, Lydia. Thank you so much. Talking to you has made me feel better already. I thought I'd just seem like an old fool imagining all sorts of things wrong with me and wouldn't be taken seriously. I know I've been a bit silly over this book," he tapped his medical directory. "But you believed in the palpitations even though you know what I'm like, so the doctor will too."

"I'm sure your doctor will take this seriously."

He nodded and was quiet for a minute.

"Lydia, when I said I'd been silly, you didn't say, 'oh no you're not, Mr Thirwall.' Have I been very annoying?"

"Not exactly annoying, it's just I hate to see you worried over nothing."

"Like my deadly rash?" he asked, grinning.

I smiled, remembering the horrible disease that was nothing more than the pattern of his knitted vest pressed into his skin where he'd been sitting still for so long.

"Yes, like that."

"It's a wonder you put up with it all."

I showed him the green colouring and told him the use I'd briefly considered putting it to.

He laughed so hard I couldn't help joining in.

"What did your doctor say, Mr Thirlwall?" I asked the following week.

"It's Taff, I keep telling you."

"OK," I agreed. "What did your doctor say?"

"Nothing."

"What do you mean, nothing?" I demanded, outraged. "This could be serious, that's not right …"

"Lydia, it's OK," he interrupted. "My doctor was away. I saw this girl instead. When she said she was a doctor, I hardly believed her. It seemed like she should be at school."

I smiled; I'm half his age, but even I've noticed that doctors and police officers are starting to look younger.

"When she started examining me, I changed my mind sharpish."

"She did a good job then?" I asked, as we waited for the kettle to boil.

"I'll say. Gave me a good look over. Asked loads of questions then got out her stethoscope and listened to my heart. Everything it said in my book, she did."

"So, what is causing your palpitations?" I asked.

"She said it's probably due to introspection," he said solemnly.

"What's that? Can they cure it?"

He laughed. "I have to cure it myself. It just means I'm sitting around listening to my heart beat and getting in a state if it changes."

I laughed too; I'd panicked at the sound of a long word without stopping to think what it meant.

I made the tea and sat down. "But you really do have the palpitations?"

"Well, I get the odd slightly irregular beat. Lots of people do, the doctor said and usually it's nothing to worry about."

"So, how does she know you haven't got anything worse than a chronic dose of introspection?"

"She doesn't. Not yet. They're doing tests just to be on the safe side, but she said anxiety is probably the cause. It makes sense because, as you know, I have been worrying about my health lately."

"Just a bit."

"Well, the doctor said sitting around getting bored isn't good for me. I've decided to join the bowls club and my neighbour has somehow talked me into going to tea dances."

"Well, that's great! I'm sure it'll do you good."

"There is one snag."

"What's that?"

"If I'm off out all the time, I'm not sure I'll be able to manage all the housework."

"I suppose I could manage a bit of cleaning in between my tea breaks, Mr Thirlwall."

"It's Taff."

"I'll try to remember."

4. No Healthy Options

Rhiannon looked at the buffet table with despair. Every option involved white bread or pastry, with just an occasional slice of tomato or sprinkle of cress here and there to brighten it up. Admittedly the creamed salmon sandwiches, cheese straws and mini quiches were popular with most members, but…

"What about people who are vegan, suffer allergies or are just trying to keep their weight down?" she'd asked Angela, who was in charge of catering, when she'd attended her first event in the social club.

"You're lovely and slim."

"Thank you, but that's not …" She was left talking to herself as Angela went to fetch a tray of pork pies. Something similar happened whenever Rhiannon tried to raise the subject.

This time, Angela just shook her head and said, "I don't hold with all these silly fads."

"It's not silly! Some people have health issues or ethical concerns and …" Once again she was speaking to Angela's back.

"What's up, love?" asked Cath. "Regretting letting me talk you into joining the committee?"

Cath was a customer of the health food store Rhiannon owned. She'd overheard Rhiannon and her daughter arguing.

"I'm supposed to be the manager, Mum and you're supposed to be semi-retired. It's not fair you being in here all day everyday double checking everything I do! Get yourself a hobby or something, can't you?"

"Why not join me on the social club committee?" Cath had suggested.

At first it seemed the ideal solution, but Rhiannon quickly realised being a regular committee member officially only took up two hours once a month. Even so, Rhiannon had her photo on the wall along with the officials who had more interesting and time consuming roles.

"I'm really worried that Angela will upset some groups by not providing suitable food, or worse, cause someone to have a serious allergic reaction because she doesn't take restricted diets seriously," Rhiannon explained.

"Hmm, yes with you being on the committee that would look bad for your health food business. It's the AGM very soon. If you offered to take charge of the catering, you could see it was done right."

"I did think of that, but I've been looking back through the records. Once people get roles like that they keep hold of them. I don't know how you got me added to the committee – it's been exactly the same people for years."

"That's not always a good thing."

"No. Too many things here are done in the same way just because they've always been done that way." Rhiannon didn't go on, as one of the things which infuriated her was the way Cath took the minutes of their meetings.

"Tell me about it! Those minutes… But that's how I was shown and I don't know a better way."

Rhiannon made a few suggestions.

"I knew a business woman like you would know how it should be done!"

"And because of my business I know about healthy eating."

"Of course you do! Don't worry, I'll propose you at the AGM."

"That's kind," Rhiannon said. She didn't want to seem ungrateful by pointing out that someone would need to second her and even then there would need to be a vote. Still, perhaps just by showing Angela that her position wasn't entirely safe she'd manage to get her to make a few changes.

At the AGM the minutes of the previous one were read out and agreed as correct, probably because nobody understood them well enough to disagree. Then came the election of the officers. Different people proposed the re-election of the existing chairperson, her deputy, and the treasurer. Rhiannon wasn't surprised they were voted in unanimously, as that's what always happened.

"Now we come to the position of catering manager..." the chairperson said.

"I propose Rhiannon Crosby," Cath said.

"I second that," Angela declared.

Before Rhiannon could take that in, she was not only unanimously elected, but Angela had proposed her as secretary, Cath seconded it, and she was voted into that role as well.

"These are for you," Cath said afterwards, handing over her notes for the minutes.

"And so is this," said Angela, offering her a plate of the most delicious looking salad. "It seemed the least I could do."

"I don't understand what's just happened," Rhiannon said, although she was beginning to guess. When the treasurer handed out the financial statements she'd noticed purchases from the local greengrocer. Clearly Angela could and did produce healthy food – she'd just hidden that from Rhiannon.

"I'm afraid you've been handed something of a poison chalice, my dear," Cath explained. "Once you're on the committee the only way off it, unless you want a huge scandal which wouldn't be good for your business, is to die, or find someone else to take your place."

5. Why Doesn't She Get Any Help?

"Mum, I'm going jogging. Want to cycle with me?" Danny asked.

"You're old enough to go out on your own." He used that excuse to disappear whenever Ellie wanted him around. Always leaving her home alone he was, which wasn't fair now it was just the two of them. No wonder she'd turned to comfort eating and gained weight. Now she was trying to do something about it he, and the rest of the world, seemed determined to sabotage her efforts.

The media confused her about what was healthy. One day a vegetable was a superfood, the next it wasn't better than any other. Dark chocolate and red wine were good for you, but you weren't supposed to consume much. Ellie mostly ate foods labelled 'low calorie' or 'reduced fat'. They weren't nice, but she dutifully chomped through. Right now it was sugarless biscuits.

"I thought it would help if we exercised together," her son said.

It might help him, but Ellie needed someone to help her. She rang a friend.

"There's Zumba in the village hall in half an hour. See you there?" Sue suggested.

"What? No! It's impossible to park and there's no café."

"It takes less than ten minutes to walk and no café is…"

"If I can't get a healthy snack afterwards I'll just buy chocolate. You know what I'm like."

"Yes, I do."

"Then why won't you help me?"

"I'm trying. OK, the gym it is."

The drive was stressful. Ellie munched through mints at every red light in an effort to keep her blood pressure down.

"How can I help you?" the receptionist asked.

"What's available?" Ellie asked.

"Right now, everything, except for static bikes."

"That's what I wanted to use!"

"Really?" her friend asked. "It's a boring and expensive way to do something you can do yourself."

"I don't want to do it by myself. Besides, those bikes show how many calories you've burned."

"So do the treadmills," the receptionist pointed out.

Ellie tried, but hers was broken. After puffing away for absolutely ages it only registered 27, so that was no help.

Oh well, if you want something done, do it yourself. Ellie went to the self service café and helped herself to a nice gooey cake.

6. You Just Have To Try

Trish was just a little anxious during the night. It was the first time her children had been on a sleepover, so that was to be expected. Her worries intensified when her phone rang quite early that morning, but vanished the moment she heard her sister-in-law's cheerful greeting. Laura asked if the boys could stay all day. After hearing they were having fun and excited to have woken in a different room and be eating waffles instead of their usual breakfast, Trish happily agreed.

Trish had always been on the nervous side, but it hadn't really held her back. Nerves didn't stop her getting a part-time job she enjoyed, meeting and marrying the love of her life, and giving birth to three boys she adored. But could she be holding the children back? Toby was trying to teach them to ride bikes, but she'd warned them so many times to be careful they lacked the confidence to go fast enough to stay upright. He took them paddling in the sea, but as soon as a wave brought the water above their knees they ran back to where Trish was waiting safely on dry land.

"I wish I was braver," she said at breakfast.

"You are brave – you eat my cooking," Toby joked, as he placed two pieces of extra well done toast on her plate.

"That's true!"

"And you're not afraid of thunder, the dentist, driving at night, or lots of things other people worry about."

She grinned. "Like spiders?"

"No I don't like spiders, you know I don't!" He pretended to tremble. Toby wasn't really frightened of spiders, but he wasn't keen, so it was always Trish who rescued them from the bath. She couldn't remember how it started, but now whenever he saw one (and sometimes when he hadn't) he'd leap onto a chair, or shake like a jelly and Trish and the kids would rush to save him. It always took a while as they laughed so much at his ham acting, and because they liked to inspect the spider to see which species it was and decide on the best place to release it.

"And you let the kids go on the sleepover," Toby reminded her.

She had, and clearly it had been perfectly fine. She should have known it would be. Laura would never put them in danger, and her children were unlikely do something silly, leading to them getting hurt.

"I was thinking, the kids learning to be cautious like me is probably a good thing."

"Oh?" Clearly that thought had never occurred to Toby.

"They don't rush up to strange dogs or lark about by the water's edge putting themselves in danger like some do."

"No."

"But?" Although he hadn't said it, she could tell he was thinking it.

"I know you can't help worrying about things, and I know it was hard for you to agree to the kids staying at Laura's without you being there. I'm proud of you for that."

"And I'm glad you, and Laura, talked me into it. They're having a great time and once I'd accepted the idea I wasn't too concerned."

"That's good."

"But? There is something on your mind, isn't there?"

He nodded. Then leant across the table and took her hands in his. "Like you said, the kids have learned their behaviour from you. To some extent it's good they're not reckless. But, sometimes it seems more than sensible caution. They don't want to stroke friendly dogs or paddle in the sea, even when they're told it's OK."

Trish nodded. Despite what she'd told Toby, and herself, she knew he was right. They were a bit too cautious – just as she was.

Toby continued gently, "When I take them over the adventure park there are things they won't even try because they're afraid of falling."

He'd mentioned his concerns before and Trish said they'd grow out of it. She now realised that wasn't true – not if they followed her example. She'd missed out on a lot in her childhood, and still did, due to being nervous. And because her parents had been slightly overprotective, especially after the time their only child dropped her favourite doll in a river. It had immediately been swept away, and Mum and Dad had to grab Trish to stop her trying to rescue it.

"What can I do? If the kids learn not to listen to me when I'm worrying too much, they won't take any notice when what I'm saying really is important for their safety."

"I'll have a think."

"I will too."

"We could do it while we walk Buddy."

Their neighbour had injured his ankle, so Toby had been walking his big dog before and after work each day. Trish didn't go, for lots of reasons. Today being Sunday, and the kids being away, meant she was left with just one – her anxiety. Trish knew he was friendly, but he was huge. He could easily knock her down, or pull her over if she held the lead, or she might let go and he'd rush into the road and be hurt.

"You go while I clear up here and make a picnic, then we can go out for the day. I don't see why the kids should be the only ones having fun, and this might well be the last warm weekend of the year and it would be a shame to waste it."

By the time Trish heard Toby returning, she'd decided that if she could conquer one of her fears, she'd be helping her children as well as herself. Buddy should be calmer than usual, now he'd had a walk.

"Are you that eager to get going?" Toby asked when she walked up the neighbour's path as he walked down.

"I was thinking I might try stroking Buddy." She explained her idea of attempting to overcome a fear.

"That's a great idea, but not now he's back indoors. As soon as anyone picks up the lead he gets excited… Walter's friend has taken him for a drive, so Buddy would be confused and disappointed to just get a minute's attention and be shut in alone again."

"Next time then." She really would try. What Toby had said was a reason to wait, not an excuse.

As she drove them to their picnic location, Toby said, "While I was walking Buddy, I saw a van parked down by the beach. On the side it said the owner was a swimming coach. There was a lesson going on. They were obviously having fun, as despite the tide being right out, and the swimmers in up to their shoulders, I could hear laughter."

"You want the kids to have swimming lessons?"

"Maybe, but I was thinking of you. I agree that if you overcame a fear it would be good for you, and for all of us. You don't need to be able to swim for miles, but wouldn't it be great if we could all go in the water together next summer?"

"It would," she admitted. When anyone who lived further inland realised she lived within walking distance of the sea, they said how lucky she was. She always agreed, despite knowing she was wasting that good fortune.

"I looked her up online," Toby said. "She looks friendly and there are lots of comments from people saying she's patient and encouraging." He read them to Trish.

The feedback saying she'd helped improved people's stroke so much they now took part in endurance swims or won competitions alarmed Trish. Those thanking the coach for the information on safety and confidence building pep talks were a lot more encouraging. She might not be great at putting them into practise, but Trish had no problem listening to motivational talks.

She'd been to several recently, hoping she'd learn to help her boys if not herself. The theme was often along the lines of just having to believe you'd succeed and then you would. That sounded like hogwash, but one person was far more convincing. She'd said the most important thing was to try. That made sense to Trish. In most cases the things she'd not achieved in life weren't the result of her failing, but because she'd lacked the courage to try. At the time she'd promised herself she would try, the next time an opportunity presented itself.

Since then she'd managed to forget about that promise fairly often, but had attempted to walk across the glass floor in the Spinnaker Tower. OK, she only managed to put one foot on it – but for her being up that high, and looking out at the view, had also been achievements. She'd got through it all by saying to herself over and over again, 'the important thing is to try.' The boys, encouraged by her positive attitude, walked across holding Toby's hand. Afterwards she'd felt proud of herself, and was generally just a little less anxious.

Trish took a deep breath. "OK."

"You'll have swimming lessons?"

"I'll try. Do you think she'd let me book just one lesson, to see how I get on?" Trish didn't believe she'd be able to learn to swim, but if the coach really was as patient and encouraging as the feedback suggested, she might help Trish manage fearless paddling. If she could show her kids she wasn't terrified of the water, they wouldn't be either.

"Let's ask, shall we?" He immediately phoned to do that. And booked her a lesson for the following afternoon.

Toby and Trish took a leisurely stroll round a historic house, then drove on to eat their picnic lunch. There was a wide, shallow stream near where they stopped. Children where shrieking with laughter as they splashed about. It did look fun – until Trish imagined doing it herself.

After they got home, Toby said, "I'm off to walk Buddy. I'll call you when we're ready."

"Ready for what?"

"You to come and stroke him."

"But… " It was no good, she wouldn't be able to convince Toby that having booked a swimming lesson meant she didn't have to try to get close to a calm and friendly dog, after she'd suggested doing exactly that.

As soon as Toby came round the corner he stopped and told Buddy to sit. The fluffy dog obeyed immediately, and stayed sitting even when Trish reached them. That was reassuring.

"Just walk next to me," Toby said.

Trish did that, and Buddy trotted along on the other side of Toby. It was absolutely fine. She could have done that for the whole walk. Tomorrow… was her swimming lesson. Better not think about tomorrow.

"How about I switch hands and he walks between us?" Toby suggested.

"OK."

By the time they reached the gate of his home, she was close enough to Buddy that his wagging tail tickled her leg. Once in his home garden, Trish told herself to 'just try it' and put her hand on Toby's – the one which held the lead.

"Well done, love," Toby said.

He soon persuaded her to hold the lead just below his hand. "I'll still have hold of it, so you can let go any time you want."

It was OK. Buddy seemed to sense something was different and kept looking up at her while walking very slowly. "I think he's had enough now," Trish said after a couple of laps.

Toby's owner was standing in his doorway on crutches. "You're a lucky chap, Buddy. An extra bit of a walk and two people taking you."

Buddy wagged his tail furiously.

"Sit," Toby said, and bent to unclip the lead.

"Wait," Trish said. "Good boy, Buddy." She gently patted his fluffy head.

The following day Trish didn't walk Buddy with Toby because she was getting the kids ready for school, not because she was too nervous. She was very nervous about her swimming lesson, but still went.

Juliette, the swimming coach looked familiar, and clearly thought the same about Trish as she said, "I know you, I think?"

"Yes, but I'm not sure where from."

"I expect it will come to us. Now, are you ready to try going in the water?"

She very much wasn't. "Right now?"

"We'll take it slowly. We'll walk to the water's edge, and then when you feel comfortable, try getting our feet wet."

"OK."

And it was. Trish had the swimsuit she'd only ever used for sunbathing and Juliette lent her beach shoes and a bathing cap. They laughed so much at her efforts to get the thing on her head that Trish's nerves eased a little.

"We'll stop here a moment," Juliette said when the cool water barely lapped their feet, and Trish thought maybe she could have taken another small step. "We'll walk out slowly, splashing water onto our arms, then bend our knees to get our shoulders wet. Are you ready to give that a try?"

"Maybe the first part."

"Great." As they waded, OK, paddled, Juliette explained, "It's important to get in slowly. It's not really an issue today, as the sea's relatively warm, but you don't want to get cold shock."

"Do you teach all year round?"

"I usually stop at the end of October and start again in early May."

Trish was relieved. It was the last week of October, so she only had to get through today and she couldn't be asked to try again for at least six months.

To her amazement, Trish did manage to dip down and get most of her body wet – and cold! Then Trish tried floating on her back with Juliette holding under her arms. She didn't like it. Juliette told her to try to relax, but she just couldn't.

"You tried," Juliette pointed out. "It will get easier with practise."

Next Trish was asked to try moving her legs, as though swimming, but with Juliette holding her up. That was better. At least she didn't go rigid, so was able to attempt the movements Juliette described. She had another try.

"You're getting it!" Juliette said.

"Really?" It had felt as though Juliette was doing less to hold her up, and Trish was helping herself to float.

"Definitely. I could feel you moving forward. Did it feel better?"

Trish admitted it had. She'd felt safe with Juliette holding her, so had been able to concentrate on kicking her legs. That concentration had stopped her worrying so much. As Trish got changed she started to shiver a little with cold, but also felt a buzz from what she'd achieved. She started to believe she could overcome her fear enough to enjoy paddling with her children – and to stop them learning to be as scared as she previously was.

When Juliette said, "This Indian summer can't go on much longer, shall we say the same time tomorrow?" she'd only hesitated a moment. A small part of her wanted to put off the next lesson until it was too cold. A bigger part of her was keen to keep trying.

At home that evening, Trish spoke enthusiastically about her lesson. The children seemed interested, and then delighted when she lay across the footstool with Toby holding her up, and demonstrated the leg kicks. They all laughed a lot as the whole family took turns, and Trish was sure her children would be happy learning to swim.

Trish was still enthusiastic and optimistic the next morning at work, when her colleagues asked how she'd got on. Then one of them looked Juliette up online. "Wow! She's swum the channel. That's incredible."

Trish agreed. Juliette was something special. That thought made Trish remember where she'd seen Juliette before. She was the speaker at one of the motivational talks Trish had heard. That meant Juliette was confident on land as well as in the water. Not an ordinary person with weaknesses and fears like Trish. Except Trish's fears weren't ordinary.

As soon as Trish arrived for her second lesson, Juliette waved a plastic tub at her.

"I've made brownies as a reward for when you've swum a little bit."

"You'll be eating them all then!"

"What's wrong?"

Trish tried to explain, but only got as far as mentioning the talk.

"I remember that! I was terrified."

Trish seriously doubted that. "Really? It didn't show."

"Not giving the actual talk. Before that I was shown into a back room to get ready. I walked in and ran out when I spotted a humungous spider – almost knocked some poor woman down. I was a wreck, but calm as you like she said, 'Don't worry, I'll get it.' She marched straight in, picked it up and then called me to open a window so she could put it outside. I couldn't even look at her. Oh! Was that you?"

"I'd forgotten about that." To her it was no big deal, but clearly it had made an impression on Juliette.

"Thanks for helping me out. I saw how brave you were and thought of what I was about to tell the audience – that you can do things if you try. I calmed down enough to do the talk, then signed up for a course to get over my fear."

"Did it work?"

"It's starting to."

"Spiders are fascinating creatures when you learn about them," Trish assured her. "I guess I need to learn more about swimming." If Juliette had fears she could overcome thanks to Trish's example, then the same would be true of her fantastic children. They were worth stepping out of her comfort zone and getting a bit chilly for.

An hour later Trish was warming up with a cup of tea and eating a chocolate brownie. She'd earned it by swimming 'a good three metres' by Juliette's estimate. OK, she'd only done the leg part and was holding onto an enormous float, but she'd propelled herself through the water. That was a start and she'd get better, she just had to try.

The following Saturday the weather was still quite warm.

"Why don't we all go out for the day, once I've walked Buddy?" Toby suggested.

"I've got a better idea. Why don't we all walk Buddy together, and then go out?" Trish said.

"That big dog, next door?" her youngest asked, with a slight tremor in his voice.

"That's right. You know, I was a bit nervous of him before, but Daddy and I took him for a walk last week and I found out he's a big, friendly ball of fluff."

"Really fluffy?"

"Really, really fluffy. When I patted his head my hand sunk in this far! Maybe Daddy will let you try."

"Can we, Daddy? Can we?" the children asked.

Toby, looking amazed, nodded.

Just wait until Trish told him that afterwards, they were going back to that picnic spot by the wide, shallow stream and she would be taking towels to dry their feet after going for a paddle. All of them together.

7. Tidying Up

I'd felt reasonably confident as I checked my watch. Yes! I'd completed five miles in a fraction under my personal best. If you're a runner I doubt you'd be the slightest bit impressed with my time, but two months ago I'd have been shattered after walking that far so had no doubts I was now considerably fitter than I'd been for months. No, fitter than I'd been for years. Perhaps even fit enough to sign up for Marc Rossini's exercise classes.

Getting fit enough for fitness training sounds a bit daft, doesn't it? But given my couch potato lifestyle and the fact they were 'high intensity rapid results interval training with attitude' it was definitely a sensible move. Of course I could have signed up for relaxing stretch and tone, zen yoga or even beginner's aerobics and not needed the preparation, but none of those were run by Marc Rossini, a man I'd had crush on for years. In any case the whole thing was down to my sister.

Like I said, a few months back I was something of a couch potato. Appropriately enough, spuds were just about the only vegetable I'd eaten in a while and I looked rather like one. My sister was always trying to get me out in the sunshine, exercising and eating properly. Knowing she only nagged because she cared, I'd walked round to her place when my day off happened to be sunny. Even back then that took me less than fifteen minutes and it struck me how lazy I'd been to always use the car for the trip.

Kerry didn't notice I hadn't driven, or even greet me properly. The first thing she'd said was, "Do me a favour and hang out the washing."

For a second it crossed my mind that was just a ploy to get me bending and stretching, but she's not usually abrupt and I saw the vacuum cleaner was out, the draining board piled with dirty crockery and the kids' attempts at pumpkin carving littered the utility area. It seemed Kerry really did need my help.

I opened the washer door, pulled everything into a basket and headed for the garden.

"Helen, wait." She rummaged through the basket, removing a few items. "Don't hang out my underwear!"

"Why not?"

"I don't want the neighbours seeing these." She held up some pretty, albeit skimpy, lingerie. "What would they think?"

Maybe at that point I didn't worry enough about what anyone thought of me, which is why I'd let myself go so badly, but Kerry was definitely at the other end of the scale. I couldn't resist teasing her. "Dunno, but if you never put any out, maybe they'll think you don't wear any."

"Oh …"

That gave her something to think about! I chuckled to myself as I hung out the rest of the load, then told her not to worry. "Of course they won't think that. Besides, with that hedge I doubt they even notice you've put anything at all on the line."

"Helen, what's happened to your car?" Kerry asked when she came in from taking the pumpkin offcuts out to the bin.

As I explained I'd voluntarily walked, I made sure no sign of my earlier amusement showed in case my good mood seemed further proof of the benefits of exercise. Then I changed the subject by asking, "What's happened to your cleaner?"

"Nothing. She'll be here in twenty minutes." Kerry switched on the vacuum before I could reply to that, so I filled the kettle and dropped teabags into mugs.

Now, if you're thinking tidying up for the cleaner is madness then we're on the same wavelength. Putting things away so she could actually clean was probably fair enough, but vacuuming? Please don't get the idea that Kerry's pampered with money to waste though, or even that she only has a cleaner to impress the neighbours. It wasn't like that. She and Pete had learned from my break-up with Danny and were trying to save their marriage.

Pete had a regular nine-to-five job with a long commute. Kerry mainly worked from home. In theory that meant choosing her own hours. In practice the school run, tackling housework when nobody was in the way, and the gradual build up of her bookkeeping business meant she was often still dealing with paid work in the evenings. As a result, even when both in the house, the two of them spent very little time properly together. She'd confessed it barely felt like a marriage. Pete's idea of getting assistance with the housework seemed to be helping. Maybe the pretty undies did too, but I didn't feel I needed that level of information.

In case you're wondering, my ex dumped me for a younger, slimmer model. That was after twelve years of Danny telling me that we were soulmates, I was gorgeous inside and out, he was the luckiest man alive, and a few months of him picking more and more faults in how I looked, dressed and behaved. You can maybe see why my few pounds excess weight became a few stone and I stopped taking any notice of what people said about me. And why Kerry and Pete decided complacency was no longer an option.

When the vacuum fell silent I said, "I've made us a cuppa. Sit down and drink it."

"I don't have time. The bathroom is a state …"

"Kerry, you're being ridiculous. The cleaner will clean it; that's her job. And if you've got time to leave your own work to scrub limescale, you've got time to sit down and have a cup of tea with your sister."

Kerry sat. "I suppose you're right. I just don't want her thinking I'm a slob."

"She knows you aren't, but would it matter so much if she did? It's only Pete's opinion you should worry about. Well, his and the kids'. And mine. Got any biscuits?"

"You can have an apple," she said.

"I don't want an apple." I fetched her biscuit tin.

"Helen, what you said about it being OK for me to worry what you think of me… That goes two ways, does it?"

"I guess." Regretfully I dropped the shortbread back in the tin and closed the lid.

Kerry squeezed my hand. "Brace yourself. I've tried being gentle and tactful but it hasn't done any good, so… I take your point that maybe I value other people's opinions a little too highly, but I have self respect too. You've practically lost yours. You're a mess."

I was shocked. She was never rude, ever. "I thought you were on my side," I said.

"I am. And I know it's just because you're down after the split with Danny and that's perfectly understandable, but I also know you're really far more like me than you admit."

"I am not."

"Really? You want to bump into Danny and *her* looking like that?"

"Of course not." In fact I didn't want to see them at all which was partly why I'd been hiding away. "OK, you're sort of right," I admitted. "I have fantasised about getting myself slim, fit and gorgeous and for him to see what he's missing."

"You've got time now you're not running around after him. Talking of running and gorgeous …"

"Don't start that again." Not that she had suggested running, but I thought I could see where she was heading.

"I didn't mean you. I was thinking of Marc Rossini. Remember him from school?"

Marc the marvellous. Marc the magnificent. Marc with the dark wavy hair, shimmering blue eyes, and gorgeous body. The reason I'd taken up cross country so I could, for a brief moment, watch his beautiful rear view as he went by. That Marc Rossini? "Yeah, vaguely. Is he back then?" I asked as casually as possible.

She handed me a leaflet for fitness classes with names like, 'Work it all Circuits', 'Fitness Fury', 'Spin Sensation', and 'Red Hot Yoga'. I didn't know what some of them were, but helpful notes such as 'high intensity' 'extreme energy', 'ultimate' and 'advanced' told me as much as I needed to know.

And the photos of lycra clad Marc, well they answered the thoughts I didn't know I had. Such as was he still as good looking as I remembered, was he still into fitness and would I still be interested in catching a glimpse of him in shorts?

I tucked the leaflet into my bag, ready to study in detail later on.

"Don't even think of signing up for any of those!" Kerry said.

"Thought you wanted me to exercise?"

"Yes, but I meant go for walks or something. These classes are for people who're already fit. I know you won't care if people see you all red-faced and sweaty or for them to know you have to stop after two minutes, but what people think isn't the problem. You could do yourself serious harm."

I didn't really care if a random stranger saw how unfit and flabby I was, but Marc Rossini would be another matter and Kerry knew it. She'd been so kind and supportive after the break-up. That's what I'd needed right after it happened. Her saying I was a mess and too unfit for exercise classes was what I needed after months of wallowing in self pity.

Despite what she says, I don't share my sister's 'what will the neighbour's think?' attitude. Mine is more 'I'll show you!' So I started with brisk walks in my lunch breaks and eating the odd piece of fruit. As I'd done nothing but eat junk and slob out, there was a quick and quite dramatic improvement.

Just as my sister knew would happen, I soon started to feel better. Each day I walked a bit further. I ate proper meals too. I started jogging in the evenings and on my days off. Soon I was quite fit. Not in a way which would make my shallow, superficial ex-husband distraught he'd lost me, but in a healthy and happy in my own skin kind of way. I went out in public, talked to people, had fun.

I completed my fastest ever five mile run one December afternoon on my day off, so I walked to Kerry's afterwards and told her how well I was doing. "And it's all thanks to you, Sis."

"I just gave you the nudge you needed, it's you who's put in the effort." She poured me the glass of water which had become my usual drink of choice. "I reckon you're fit enough for Marc Rossini's classes now."

"Quite possibly, but I won't need those; I've joined a netball team. It's more fun than gym work and I'm making friends too."

"So you haven't been exercising for him?"

"No and not for Danny either. The reason he didn't appreciate me isn't that I'd gained a bit of weight, or didn't always have time to shave my legs, but because he just couldn't appreciate a good thing when he had it. He has no loyalty, so isn't worth being upset over."

"Fantastic. I have my wonderful sister back."

"Yes you do. Let's go out and celebrate."

"With mineral water and green salad?" It was a fair question as that's what I'd eaten the last few times we'd gone out together.

"No, tea and cake," I said. Healthy eating is a very good thing, but becoming obsessed over it isn't.

"You're on. When?"

"Now?" I suggested.

"The cleaner is coming at three."

I glanced at my watch. Twenty minutes to go. "I'll chuck those magazines in the recycling and wash up. You shove all the kid's stuff in the cupboard under the stairs," I said. "No vacuuming though!"

"Deal."

I still think it's slightly daft of her to worry that the cleaner might think she's untidy, but that's my sister for you. I don't want her to change. It might seem she'd wanted me to, but she hadn't. Danny had. He'd wanted a level of perfection which doesn't exist. Kerry just wanted me happy and healthy – a wish we all share for those we truly love.

8. Puppy Love

Monday morning Robin has splodged toothpaste on his tie. It's sooo minty fresh, surely he'll notice? But no, he's totally oblivious.

Can't let your man go out like that, can you? Some women, Susannah for example, might decide to look after him 'properly'. I don't want that. Neither should he. A woman who does every little thing wouldn't be good for Robin.

As I'm not about to rush around with a sponge and clean his tie, Robin will have to deal with it. Not being one to nag, I give the end a playful tug.

"What are you doing, Melody?" he asks, pulling it away from me. "Oh, I've spilled something. Hmm, toothpaste. Wait here, I'll change it."

It doesn't take long and we're soon off to work. Six-foot, broad shouldered Robin works in customer service for a catalogue clothing company. I don't get why people find that hard to believe. Mind you, some think that as I'm blonde and cute all I need do is sit in the corner looking pretty.

Typical day in the office really. Bex and other sensible members of staff call 'good morning' as we arrive. Susannah ignores me and gets all touchy feely with Robin. Honestly he put his coat on himself, I'm pretty sure he can take it off and hang it up.

"I need coffee," Robin says as though he hadn't had one when he got out of bed and another with his cornflakes. "Anyone else?"

"I'll make it. You sit just here," Susannah says, pushing him into the seat beside her.

I'm not at all surprised when Susannah returns with nothing for me other than a view of her bum as she drapes herself across his desk. Neither am I surprised when Bex brings me water, which is all I drink, when she fetches her own coffee.

Robin has a constant stream of calls and gently flirts with several customers. "I bet you'll look sensational in it, once we get the right size sent out," he says.

It's just a bit of friendly chat to turn someone with a complaint into a loyal customer.

As it's a typical day, Robin eats his second chocolate bar before lunchtime. Mmm chocolate. It smells sooo good. He must feel me watching as he says, "Sorry, none for you."

"Were you talking to me?" Susannah asks, oh so sweetly.

"To Melody. Chocolate isn't good for her."

"How about me, Robin?" Susannah rests her hand on his arm. "Will you give me a taste of something sweet?"

I want to snarl as he offers the bar, but resist. Then Robin gives what's left to Bex and I see Susannah's hackles raise. That's sooo funny.

"Too much junk food isn't good for you either, Robin," Susannah purrs, like a cat who's sheathed the claws she hopes to dig into him later. "Why don't I fetch you something from the deli?"

I'm not putting up with that! I give him a nudge to remind him I'm there.

"No thanks, Susannah. Melody likes to get out at lunchtime …"

Bex joins the queue a few places behind us. Unlike Susannah would, she doesn't push in to join us. Unlike with Susannah, I wouldn't mind if she did. To Bex, Robin is a man, not prey to play with and torment. There I go, referring to Susannah as catty again. Well, she is.

Robin buys a cheese sandwich for himself and I get ham. Mmmmm ham tastes sooo good.

After work we walk home the long way. I like doing that. Unlike chocolate, exercise is good for me. And Robin of course. Once we're home there's the usual chores, then dinner. It's beef tonight. Yummy. After that we snuggle on the sofa and listen to music. It feels sooo good.

Tuesday morning Robin has his jumper inside out. I'm wondering how to tell him, when he puts on his coat and says it's time to go.

We arrive at work before anyone but Bex is there.

"Your jumper is inside out," she says. That's it, just a tactful word. No tugging it over his head, turning it round and smoothing it down over his body as cat features, sorry, Susannah would have.

"I need coffee," Robin says. Maybe he does, he only had one this morning. "Want one, Bex?" he asks.

"Oh, yes… thanks."

I like her, I really do. She's nice, thoughtful, sensitive and a bit shy. Rather like Robin… I'm sooo dumb! Susannah's blatant seduction attempts and Robin's polite resistance blinded me to the truth! It's clear now. They, Bex and Robin, are falling in love, oh so tentatively. One nudge in the wrong direction could keep them apart. Go the other way and they'll realise their true feelings. Drastic action is required!

All morning I watch. What can I do? I can't say anything. I can't push her down the stairs. Well, I could but if anyone realised I'd done it deliberately I'd be out of a job and out of Robin's life.

At lunchtime it's off to the deli again. Robin and Bex use it most days and although I'd not realised before, they must hope to bump into each other there. The place is always busy, so that's not as easy as it sounds.

It's not until we're leaving that I get my idea. I lunge towards Bex, dragging Robin with me. Instinctively he puts an arm out to stop himself falling. Equally instinctively, she reaches for him.

"Bex?" he says as their bodies collide.

"Robin," she murmurs as she holds him steady.

"Bex," he whispers into her hair.

They could have let go of each other by now, without falling over, but they haven't. I'm temporarily forgotten in all this, which is just as well. A guide dog in harness should never make a sudden move like that. I won't do it again, I promise. But just this once, it seemed sooo right.

9. Five A Day

Every day if you chomp or crunch
An apple and a pear, or munch any
Two sweetly crispy, juicy pieces of

Flavoursome fruit after lunch
Include three or more
Vegetables – make room for mushrooms
Enjoy endive in salad or even coleslaw

Parsnips, peppers or pumpkins, (not potatoes)
Onions are fine, asparagus sublime
Radish and cabbage, spinach too
Tomatoes fresh or sun-dried or frozen
In cans or juiced are good for you
Oranges, Orach, oriental greens
Nectarines are nice and peaches are peachy
Squash in some squashes and be full of beans

Artichokes to Zea maize are great, even

Dried like dates and sultanas
Apricots, prunes and bananas -
You'll be healthy if you do as I say.

One scoop of peas, a head of calabrese
Five ripe strawberries

Fill your plate with spring greens
Roast a few aubergines
Up your veggie intake
Increase your fruit consumption
To be slimmer and stronger

And maybe live longer
Nibble crudités, slurp down smoothies
Don't skimp on the good stuff

Vitamins, minerals and fibre
Each bite contains, so ensure you
Get your fair share!

10. Absolutely Nothing

"What would you like for your birthday, love?" David asked.

Without hesitation, Helena replied, "Absolutely nothing."

"I really meant what do you want to do? What kind of party?"

"Same answer."

"Oh come on, don't be like that," he coaxed. "Turning fifty is nothing to be ashamed of, especially if you look as good as you do."

"Thank you, but I wasn't fishing for compliments and I'm not bothered if people know my age."

"That's OK then. So, what kind of party? Fancy dress, or something a bit more classy?"

Helena had hoped to spend the evening relaxing at home. She supposed that she should see her family, preferably a few at a time, during the day. Afterwards she'd like it to just be her and David. They could have a takeaway pizza and bottle of wine. No fuss, no stress, no washing up – well the wineglasses, she wasn't going to drink out the bottle, but her husband could wash them. It was her birthday after all.

David had celebrated his fiftieth the year before and she'd organised a big party for him. It took a lot of effort. She'd tracked down old school friends of David's as well as inviting his work colleagues, running club friends, quiz team and of course their extended family. Finding somewhere large enough to hold everyone, helping those who needed it book accommodation, and organising all the food and drink, plus a band, had been exhausting and stressful. She hadn't minded though, because she'd known it was exactly what David wanted.

The evening itself had been fun as far as she could recall. Tiredness had made it a bit of a blur. Helena wouldn't have minded if a surprise party had been organised for her, but with just six weeks to go that clearly wasn't going to happen.

She tried again to explain that she was happy to mark the occasion, and that her preferred way of doing it would be to do nothing at all. No planning beforehand, no fuss on the day, no clearing up afterwards, would all add up to the perfect birthday gift.

"How about a spa day?" David suggested.

"Actually, that's not a bad idea." Getting fussed over and pampered wasn't something which would usually interest her particularly. However the idea of not even having to decide what to wear and just lounging around in a robe, listening to soothing music and being anointed with fragrant potions was quite appealing.

Also, as it would cost quite a bit, she could ask her family to chip in rather than buy gifts. That way she wouldn't have to be grateful for the chocolates her daughters bought and then ate. Neither would she need to fake delight at the hideous clothes her mother-in-law would probably buy her.

"You need bringing up to date," she'd declare as she handed Helena a selection of items which were too bright, too short and far too tight. She might be right about them being fashionable though; retro was in, wasn't it? Last year's offering had been a lemon yellow crop top and Paisley patterned Capri pants.

"The girls could come with you," David said. "Make a nice girly day of it."

She loved her daughter's, but being enclosed with the two of them for a whole day would be dreadful. Evie would go on and on about her wedding plans – conveniently and completely forgetting that Helena was the one who'd be doing all the actual work involved with whichever of her elaborate ideas she eventually selected. Sasha would get jealous and try to monopolise Helena's attention and then the sisters would work their way up to a full scale row.

"On second thoughts I'd rather spend the day at home," Helena told him.

Unfortunately he passed that information on to his mum.

"She can't spend the day moping," her mother-in-law said. "We'll come over and cheer her up. Maybe we could make a start on the redecorating. All those pale colours you have are so dull, I know just what your house needs."

Of course once Helena's own parents realised David's were visiting, they felt they should too.

"It's such a long way and so inconvenient, but if that's what you want, dear," Mum said.

Helena could hardly say she didn't, even though it meant they'd stay at least three nights and it would mean so much more work for her. Dad had a weird medical complaint, the chief symptom of which was not being able to eat whatever anybody else was having. He also had strong political opinions which he didn't keep to himself. Strong opinions not shared by David's parents.

Evie announced she and 'my darling fiance' would also stay for a few days.

"I'm coming, Mum," Sasha declared. "But I don't see why Evie should have a bedroom and not me though, just because she's turned into Bridezilla."

Helena didn't see why she and David should sleep on the sofa bed, but they probably would, just to keep the peace. Besides, thanks to the stomach cramps she'd been suffering lately, she'd be uncomfortable wherever she slept.

"Did I mention the problem with the cat?" her mother asked the day before she and Dad were due to arrive.

"No, I didn't even know you had a cat."

"Oh, it's not ours. The neighbours asked us to look after it for a few days. Normally I'd have said no, but as we're coming to you I knew it would be OK. It's mostly no trouble she says, except for scratching the furniture, but you will have to keep it away from your father because of his allergies."

Another stomach pain gripped Helena, leaving her without the strength to reason with her mother. The pains been getting worse and more frequent since David first tried to persuade her to do something special for her birthday. Why hadn't she suggested a weekend in Paris? It wouldn't have been much trouble to book and pack for that. Too late now.

Her sister-in-law rang up the next day. "About your birthday, Helena. I'd love to join in, but just say if it's not convenient. I can easily come another day."

"No, please do come." Lynne was the ideal guest. She was sensible and charming with no special dietary requirements, and a talent for getting on with people. Best of all she had a campervan, so didn't require a bed or add to the queue for the bathroom. Maybe her presence would dilute some of the annoyances.

Helena woke up on her birthday with a cat on her face and pain in her belly. She hoped she wasn't getting like her father, with all his imaginary problems. There couldn't be anything actually wrong as the pain was in a different place each time. Probably just stress.

She waited for her turn to use the bathroom, then went back down to a big pile of cards and presents – and a house full of people expecting breakfast.

"I'd have done it but I didn't want to interfere," her mother-in-law said.

To be fair Helena did hate people interfering as she cooked and would rather do it herself than have help from her mother-in-law, or the very begrudging help of her daughters or Mum fussing around getting in the way.

"Everyone want a full English?" Helena asked.

"A fried egg sandwich would do me love," David said.

"And me, Mum. I've seen this wonderful wedding dress, but I'll need to lose a few pounds," Evie said.

Helena waited for Sasha to agree to that with too much enthusiasm, but was pleasantly surprised when all she said was, "You've got plenty of time, don't fret."

Dad did check the bread was wholemeal and the eggs free range, but thankfully everyone agreed a fried egg sandwich would be just fine.

As Helena buttered every slice of bread and cracked every egg in the house, she realised her family were being less demanding than usual. Maybe they hadn't realised they were causing her so much stress by all being there, and simply wanted to share her special day. They were making an effort to be nice to each other too. Her father-in-law hadn't responded to Dad's thoughts on the Labour party leadership and Dad had taken the hint and began talking about organic vegetables.

"I don't use any chemicals on my allotment," her father-in-law said. "And you're quite right that the flavour is better."

It really did seem as though it was all going to be bearable, and Helena had almost convinced herself she wasn't in pain when the cat jumped onto the counter, knocking the gift wrapped present from Lynne onto the floor where it smashed.

David grabbed the cat and shut it in the lounge, but not before anyone had noticed it lick the butter.

"I hope you won't be using that butter to cook the eggs," Mum said.

"No, of course not." They were already sizzling in both her frying pans and on the griddle. "I've used olive oil."

"I can't eat that," Dad said. "It gives me a rash."

The pain as Helena sliced him some cheese instead was so intense she could almost imagine she'd thrust the knife into her abdomen rather than the block of cheddar.

"There you go," she reached over Sasha to put Dad's plate on the table.

"Yuck, your breath sEviels awful," Sasha said.

"Don't be so nasty!" David snapped.

"If Sasha hadn't hogged the bathroom for hours, Mum could have brushed her teeth," Evie said. "But of course she never thinks of anyone but herself."

"You can talk with your non stop wedding drivel!"

"Stop it the pair of you!" David yelled.

"There's no need to shout," Helena's mother-in-law screamed.

"I think I'm getting a migraine," Dad informed them.

"I'm only telling the truth, it's all weird like pear drops," Sasha whined.

Helena vaguely remembered that breath like pear drops was a symptom of something just before she sank away into a faint.

As she drifted in and out of consciousness, Helena was aware of David holding her hand, her sister-in-law Lynne calmly explaining the situation over the telephone and almost everyone else shouting.

"Someone call an ambulance."

"No, I'll drive her to hospital."

"Not after what you drank last night. I keep telling you about that but you never listen."

"It's because she eats the wrong things. Her health is delicate like mine."

"Hot sweet tea, that's what she needs. It's good for shock."

"No, she shouldn't have anything in case she needs an operation," Helena's sister-in-law said. "I think she may have appendicitis."

Helena just had time to realise Lynne was right, before passing out again. She didn't remember much else until she came round from the operation.

"You're going to be fine," the doctor said after describing the procedure he'd just performed. "There may be some discomfort, but I'll give you something for that."

"Thank you." Although she'd yet to unwrap any of the others, Helena was fairly sure that injection was the best birthday present she would get. The pain and her worries just melted away in a matter of moments.

"Normally we only allow two visitors at a time and only for short periods, but I see today is a special occasion and there are a lot of people in the family room. I could make an exception?"

Helena wasn't sure if she could really hear them all bickering, or imagined it. "No doctor, please don't do that. I'd much rather just lie here quietly."

The doctor nodded understandingly. Even if she'd not heard them it seemed he had. "I'll tell them you're fine, but need to be left alone to recover, shall I?"

"Thank you."

A few minutes later David arrived at her bedside, alone.

"Are you OK, really?" he said after kissing her.

"I will be. Where is everyone?"

"Lynne is going to feed them and send them home."

Helena felt as though she'd been given another shot of whatever had been in the doctor's syringe. "Thank her for me and say she's given me the best gift of all."

"But hers got broken and the others are still wrapped up at home. You've had absolutely nothing."

"Exactly."

11. Just A Trim

A glance in the mirror shows Iris she looks as fed up as she feels. Talk about a bad hair day! She's conditioned it and combed it and blowed it and ruffled it but the result is a mess. A mess with strong hints of grey. It's time for serious action. She sighs. A light trim is all she ever has and usually all she ever wanted, but a light trim isn't going to be enough now.

Iris tries some of the lipstick she'd bought that was half price and far too bright. Now she looks fed up with an artificial smile, but at least she has a smile.

Jim is his usual uncommunicative self over breakfast. He mutters his thanks as she hands him his toast, but she doubts he'd have noticed if she'd dyed her hair to match the lipstick. Jim aims a kiss at her as they each leave for work. His lips brush her ear and he's gone, without a word.

There's plenty of conversation on the bus. No one speaks to Iris, but she can listen, just as she'd listened to the conversation on the way home yesterday.

"Hey, your hair looks great, really glam," one sleek-haired girl had told another.

"Thanks. My fella lurves it, he took me out to a fancy restaurant then clubbing just to show me off. After the difference going red made to you, I knew I should go for something radical."

"You said it'd make a difference, but I didn't know it'd make that much of a difference. I went and asked for a pay rise yesterday – and got it!"

"I'm not surprised, not really. My sister's a new woman since she had her hair cut short."

"No way! She had such lovely long blonde hair."

"Yes, but it didn't do her much good. She'd never do anything active because it took her so long to wash and dry it afterwards and if she went out in the wind or rain it soon looked a wreck. She'd turned into a spotty couch potato. Since having it cut, she's been swimming regularly and joined a Badminton club. She's lost two stone and gained a boyfriend. They're in lurve."

"Good for her."

"The right style can change your life."

"Guess you're right about that."

Iris guessed then that she had the wrong style, that's if she had a style at all. All night she'd thought about it and by this morning she'd been sure she had to change her hair if she was to change her life. She looks around in vain for the girls with the gorgeous hair. No bus journey to the supermarket job for them. They're probably travelling to a high powered business brunch, or being whisked away for a spontaneous break with the boys who 'lurve' them. Maybe they are having a deep and meaningful conversation or perhaps the redhead is being brave and the blonde is proving those with fair hair really do have more fun. Whatever they're doing, Iris doubts they're being ignored or taken for granted.

At work she's asked to supervise the cheese counter yet again. If her hair was red would she insist it was her turn for the warmth of the bakery or the scent of the floristry department? As she slices large blocks of cheddar into smaller portions, Iris studies her customer's hair and tries to imagine the advantages and disadvantages of each style.

A tight perm would be easy to look after and give her more time in the mornings, but as that was how her mother wore hers, might make her feel she'd turned into her overnight. Longer styles could look elegant, but would be a problem at work. She doesn't mind wearing a cap, but doesn't fancy stuffing a bulging hair net into one. Maybe she should shave it incredibly short like those two girls in their dungarees and sensible shoes? Even her Jim might notice that. No; to have the right hairstyle, she needs to keep some hair.

At home, Iris experiments with grips and bands in front of the bathroom mirror.

There's a tap on the door and Jim asks, "You all right in there?"

She lets him in. "Do you think I have the wrong hairstyle?"

"No love, I think it suits you," Jim says as he pulls out the last hair grip and smoothes her fringe.

"It's getting boring though. I always just have a light trim. That's what the girl who does it expects me to have and I'm never brave enough to ask for anything else."

"Have it done somewhere else then."

"But the only other salon in town is very expensive."

"I've noticed you've been looking a bit fed up. You go and have anything you like done; my treat. The change might do you good and if you don't like it, well it'll grow out soon enough."

Bless him, he had noticed then.

When she books the appointment she confesses she doesn't know what she wants done. The chirpy girl says that's no problem, Iris can come in early, look at some style books and have a chat with a consultant.

Iris walks past the salon three times. Shop staff further along the street are busy bringing in signs and taking down displays. Watching one girl struggling to manoeuvre a large tray of pre-packed bacon through a narrow doorway, Iris is pleased she doesn't have to do that at the supermarket. She's still too early for her appointment so takes another trip down the High Street. The girl she'd seen earlier locks the door of the butcher's shop and pulls off her cap. Shiny blonde hair tumbles out. Iris isn't sure if she's the girl from the bus, but her hair is just as lovely once she's shaken it free and run her fingers through it.

As Iris approaches the salon, an elderly couple walk out arm in arm. Her sparse white hair is neatly arranged in tight curls and he's telling her how lovely she looks.

She smiles and says, "Thanks love, but you'd say that whatever I had done."

"That's because you'll always be lovely to me."

Iris is ushered to a comfy leather sofa and given style books by a glamorous brunette in head to toe skinny black. The models are all very young and their styles much more extreme than anything Iris would have worn even when she'd been their age. Maybe she can just change the colour a bit instead of the style?

Iris puts down the style book and picks up a leaflet advertising 'hairometherapy – An indulgent deep conditioning treatment and massage to really make the most of your hair's natural shine and body and complement your chosen style'.

Next, she looks at the colour charts. Red might make her braver, but does she want to be? Everyone at work loves her easygoing nature and because she never complains about extra shifts on the cheese counter, no one minds her taking a quick extra tea break to warm her hands. Her Jim is a gentleman, but he isn't likely to prefer her as a blonde as he already loves her. She could choose a rich brown, but then she'll have paler roots and look as though she has more grey than is really there. A deeper or brighter shade might make her look washed out. Lightening it seems pointless as that's happening naturally anyway. She'll stick to her natural colour.

What style then? Shorter slicker hair would mean she'd save time in the mornings, but she's long since learnt that Jim is never at his best before his first mug of tea and to be honest neither is she. Iris is used to her morning ritual with the big brush and hairdryer, she enjoys treating herself to scented conditioners and other fancy products whenever her store has a special offer. This is the style her grandchildren have always known, the look she'd had when she was accepted for her job and which Jim says suits her.

"So, have you decided what you'd like done?" asks the consultant.

"Just a light trim all over… and the hairometherapy please." She settles back for a bit of pampering and a nice chat with the stylist, confident Jim will tell her she looks lovely as soon as she gets home.

12. Wandering Hands Disease

"What are you doing, Nigel?" Lauren giggled and moved his hand back to her waist.

"I told you there were advantages to going out with a medical student; this is one of them."

She gave him a look over the top of her 'medicinal' glass of red wine. "You mean I get to play doctors and nurses with you?"

"Lauren! How can you say that? This is entirely for the good of your health, you know. I'm giving you the benefit of a full and thorough private examination."

"You seem to be examining some bits rather more thoroughly than others," she replied and again repositioned his hand. "I suppose you've got some clever reason for that?"

"Indeed I have. Right now, I'm checking to see if you have swollen lymph glands."

"And have I?"

"I won't know until I've examined you, will I?"

"I suppose so… Hey! Are you sure I've got lymph glands there?"

"Positive. They occur throughout the body."

"So why aren't you examining my feet?"

"Well, there are areas of the body where the lymph glands are grouped together in chains. These include the armpits, groin and head and neck."

"Oh! I remember that when I was little, my granny used to say about my glands being up when I had tonsillitis or a cold. Is that the same thing?"

"Yes. It's common for the lymph glands to swell after an infection. If you had an infection in your throat then the glands on your neck would be the ones infected. And if you had an infection just here," he said moving his hand across her tight, pink sweater, "the ones in your armpit would be the ones that were swollen."

"Gerrof and explain this properly. You've got me interested – and no claiming you've got an infection somewhere and wanting me to feel whatever is swollen up."

"Lauren, Lauren, you've sadly misjudged me."

"Whatever."

"All right, you win." He touched her behind her ear. "Just here are your occipital lymph glands." He ran a finger down towards her neck. "Would you like me to point out your cervical lymph glands?"

"No! I'm not a medical student, but I have a good idea where my cervix is and there's no way I'm going to let …"

"You're doing it again."

"Doing what?"

"Misjudging me." He gently tapped her neck. "The cervical lymph glands are right here and down here, just above your clavicle or collar bone are the supra clavicular lymph glands and below them …" He moved his hand down.

She leant away from his touch and placed her wine on the coffee table.

"OK, I get the idea; there are lots of them all over the place. What do they do?"

"They're an important part of the immune system. The glands are connected by a network of lymph channels. Lymph is a watery fluid that forms between the cells of the body. It travels through the lymph glands, into the lymph channels and drains into the blood vessels. Both the glands and channels of fluid contain white blood cells, known as lymphocytes, and antibodies. These defend the body against infection."

"They don't seem to be protecting me from your wandering hands ..."

"I've told you, you don't need protecting from me."

"Really? Do you think I should phone my big brother for a second opinion on that?"

"Is that the big brother who's an eighteen stone scrum half for the university rugby team?"

"That's the one."

"Then no; we don't need to bother him." Nigel sat up straight, picked up the wine glasses and handed one to Lauren.

"I thought not," Lauren said after a couple of sips. "What about the lymph glands, do we need to bother about them?"

"Not usually. Most people aren't really aware of them. They're normally pea-sized and can sometimes be felt under the skin."

"Even when they're not swollen?"

"Yes."

"Can you feel mine?"

"I wouldn't like to take such a liberty; I'll keep my hands to myself."

"Are you sulking?"

"Certainly not! Just making a point."

"Oh, OK. Go on then."

He did.

She slapped his hand. "I meant go on with the explanation!"

"Ah. So sorry; my mistake." He didn't look sorry.

"The lymph glands that are under the skin become more noticeable and easier to feel if they swell. They can get to the size of a biggish marble. There are also lymph glands deeper in the chest or abdomen, but they can't be felt even if they swell."

"And they just swell when there's a nearby infection?"

"That's the most common reason. As the immune system deals with the infection the glands swell and can become tender. In that case they'll go back to normal a week or so after the infection. If the infection is a more generalised one, rather than localised, then glands all over the body could become swollen."

"Are there other reasons for them to swell?"

"Cancers could have that result. Occasionally cancers can spread to nearby lymph glands. As with an infection, the glands nearest to the site of the cancer would be affected. Lymphomas and leukaemias which are cancers of the lymphatic and blood systems might well cause a lot of glands to swell."

"Can you tell the difference between that type of swelling and one that's just due to an infection?" Lauren asked. She finished her glass of wine.

"Generally swollen lymph glands due to cancers develop more slowly than those due to infections. They also tend to be painless at first. There may not have been any infection to explain the swollen glands and they're unlikely to return to normal size as would be expected if the swelling was due to infection."

"So if I found a swollen gland and didn't know why it was swollen and it didn't go down, I should be worried?"

"I don't want you to worry about anything. Have some more wine." He refilled her glass and handed it to her. "That doesn't mean they have cancer, but it is one possibility. It's also possible that swollen glands could be caused by a reaction to drugs or as a result of another medical condition. Although these are all rare, it's better to check than to let a serious problem remain untreated. It's important for anyone who has unexplained swollen glands or glands that don't return to normal in a couple of weeks, to go and see their doctor."

"Or get a friendly medical student to give them the once over?"

"You see, I knew you'd begin to see things my way."

"Yesss, maybe. So what treatment would you suggest if you found a swelling?"

"That would depend on the cause. Obviously, until I'm fully trained if I thought you needed any kind of treatment, I'd advise you to see your GP. If you'd recently had a viral infection, then you probably wouldn't need any treatment. I'd just check to make sure the swelling went down."

"Hmm. I guess if the gland below my clavicle was swollen, you'd check on an hourly basis?"

Nigel put both of their glasses onto the coffee table. "It's important to be thorough."

"Hmm, maybe I should check yours?" She kissed his neck. "What did you say this one was called?"

13. Funny Name For A Bear

I think on some level I knew I was kidding myself. Even so I tried to believe I was safe in my bed at home. Any minute Mum would come in and tell me it was time to get up for school. Those noises I could hear where all optimistically explained away. The mechanical beepings and whirrings were Dad shaving. Footsteps were my brother hurrying downstairs.

The curtain round my bed was harder to explain. Perhaps it was to protect the sheets as my bedroom was redecorated in my favourite shade; apricot. Maybe my parents were just about to reveal the surprise. The fantasy of everything being OK was helped by the presence of B and B, my favourite teddy bear.

It wasn't so easy to pretend as the rest of the ward woke up.

The nurse called me Melanie, as she took my blood pressure. I pushed away all thoughts of the past and concentrated only on the present. I was in hospital with a broken leg. From the way I couldn't concentrate and people kept shining lights into my eyes and asking pointless questions I maybe had head injuries too. Not serious. I'm sure I correctly named the Prime Minister and the day of the week. No memory loss either, unfortunately.

There was no one who'd call me 'our little Mel' as my parents were dead. Killed by a young woman texting her friend to say she'd be with her in a few minutes. She ended up late after all, but not in the same sense of the word as

Mum and Dad. That memory was too painful, so I jumped forward to my relationship with Malcolm. He knew me so well – all my likes and dislikes. If he bought me chocolates they'd be a handpicked selection of my favourites. When we argued his words cut deep, but we rarely argued. The clothes he bought me always fitted. The holidays he booked were always to places I wanted to see. The house he choose for us was perfect.

'My Melanie' was how he always addressed me. Marvellous Malcolm, that's what I called him. Even so it didn't last. Was it too much pressure being the only person I cared about?

It was different with Simon. I hadn't overburdened him. My expectations weren't unrealistically high. If he brought me flowers they'd be pretty. It didn't matter they weren't my favourite colour.

When he took me out for a meal it was always to a nice restaurant, but never the one I'd have most liked to eat in. His gifts allowed me to have exactly what I wanted, but only because he left the choosing to me. He simply called me Mel, just as almost everyone else did.

Odd about the bear though. I've had B and B since it was bigger than me. Apparently it's a panda, although the colour scheme is the only clue. After years of me dragging it around, the shape is now closer to a penguin. Old photos show it never had the physique of any bear, but of course that didn't stop me loving it. Mum told me I named him myself, though what prompted such an odd choice, I can't say.

After our parents' death, my brother Dan and I sold the house. Well, he did. I couldn't face going back there and asked Dan to take care of the arrangements. I'd been spending a lot of time at Malcolm's flat by then anyway, so I moved in with him until the sale went through.

Dan Yell is my nickname for my big brother. That probably started as a result of my difficulty pronouncing Daniel, but it resurfaced during his moody teenage years. He'd called me all sorts. 'Smelly Melly' when I was a baby, and later when he wanted to wind me up with something other than 'Fat Belly Melly'. I was 'Yelly Melly' when I objected, and 'Telly Melly' when I complained to our parents. Usually though it was just 'Melly' and said with affection.

Dan brought my clothes and other possessions over to Malcolm's place, plus photos and a few personal belongings of our parents that he thought I'd like. He was quiet then and where I'm concerned has been practically silent since.

There wasn't room in Malcolm's flat for my parents' things, so most of it was packed into a crate and put in storage. After we split up and I started seeing Simon, Malcolm had made getting it all back unnecessarily difficult. I had to go alone and at a time to suit him. He'd tried to question me about my life without him. He said he was concerned for me. Then he'd sneeringly referred to 'Simple Simon', making it clear he knew more than I was willing to tell.

I'd been angry as I drove away. Is that why I'm in hospital? No. I remember taking the crate into my new home and reflecting that although it was precious to me and small enough that I could just about manoeuvre it unaided, Malcolm hadn't been able to make space for it. The crate is in my living room now; unopened. Except it must have been opened as B and B is here in the hospital. Simon must have done that. How odd he happened to select the one thing which would be of comfort.

Simon is simple, but only in the sense that he's uncomplicated. Uncomplicated and practical.

When he comes to visit he brings exactly the right clothes. Easy to get on over my injured leg, light enough not to add to my discomfort in the overheated ward. Everything else he brings is perfect too – the book I'd been reading, the face cream I use every morning. Not that he knows that, as I rarely let him stay over, but it's in my bathroom cabinet and there's not much else in there.

The grapes too are my favourite kind. Big black ones look nice, but sometimes the skin is bitter. These tiny yellow ones are so much sweeter. And of course the seedless kind are the more practical choice for someone in a hospital bed.

Then I remember. I had opened the crate. B and B was on top. Underneath him was the fruit bowl Dad had made when Mum persuaded him to join her in an evening class. I'd gone out to buy something to put in it. My mind had been in the past and I'd stepped out in front of a cyclist. Just an accident then. Once I learned the cyclist suffered no worse than a few bruises I was able to feel properly relieved.

Simon didn't visit many times, as I was soon discharged. I leaned on him, quite literally. He helped me get used to the crutches and drove me to appointments. I was careful not to overwhelm him as I had with Malcolm. When he offered to cook, I didn't ask him to make the food I craved, but suggested he ring for a pizza. When he asked what was wrong I said my leg was painful. Instead of allowing him to give up all his free time looking after and entertaining me, I insisted he go out with his friends.

The day after the cast was removed Simon was nervous. He was going to break up with me, I supposed. No big deal, we were never that close, but I would miss him. He was one of the good guys. I could tell that by the way he stuck around until I didn't need him anymore. As I told myself that, about losing him being no big deal, I'm sure I knew I was kidding myself. I certainly did when I realised the truth.

Simon had contacted my brother. I hadn't seen Dan in a long time. At our parents' funeral, in the solicitor's office sorting out all their paperwork and the sale of the house. When he brought B and B and the other stuff to Malcolm's flat. Not since then. Malcolm saw how distressed I became to be reminded Dan was all the family I had left, and he'd had a word.

Simon contacted my brother, after the accident. It was Dan who told him to bring B and B to me. My brother knew me before you see. Before I pushed away memories both good and bad. Before I shut down my emotions and withdrew inside myself where no one and nothing could hurt me.

Malcolm had. He'd hurt me. I'd kidded myself there too. Pretended his manipulative ways were love and compassion. Dan wasn't cut off to save me from pain, but to make me dependent on Malcolm. Yes, 'Marvellous Malcolm' knew me well enough to buy me lemon flavoured, white chocolate truffles, but he also knew how to reduce me to tears when I tried to reach out to anyone else or make decisions for myself. He controlled what I ate, how I dressed, even which house I bought with my inheritance.

Gradually I'd realised. Eventually broken free. I vowed not to make the same mistakes with Simon. I haven't. I've made fresh ones. To ensure he can't take over my life I've barely allowed him a place in it. My emotions were packed up tighter and pushed further from my mind than the memories of my parents and the happy girl I'd once been.

I made a mistake with my brother too. I should have comforted Dan and allowed him to do the same for me. There's nothing I could do to put right the past, but I did try to do better in the present and so improve the future.

We sat for hours, my brother and I, looking through old photos, recalling our childhood, rebuilding our family. There were a lot of tears, but some were happy ones. There was laughter when he remembered the kids next door laughed at the name I'd given my bear and in a misguided attempt to save me from ridicule he'd claimed it meant black and blue and set about it with felt tip pens. Fortunately they'd been the kind which washed out. On another occasion, after I'd made a disastrous attempt to bleach my hair, he'd taped yellow wool on B and B's head saying banana blonde was the latest trend. The silliness of that had cheered me up at the time and did again.

Simon was there for all of it. I let him see, let him in. Perhaps one day I'll let myself love him.

Who am I kidding? I do already.

14. The Mysterious Stone Of Ogham

Ailsa had lost something. Not just her breast and anyway that might not be permanent: she'd been offered reconstructive surgery if she wanted it. She wasn't sure she did. She'd seen quite enough of the inside of hospitals and once she was wearing one of her special bras she looked fine. She didn't exactly like her appearance without it, but she'd started to accept it and no longer shuddered if she caught sight of her naked reflection.

It was passion she'd lost. Passion for life and for her husband. She was grateful to be alive and she still loved Donald very much, but it wasn't quite the same. She missed the passion, the wanting him and being wanted in return. That wasn't something doctors could rebuild.

They'd been looking forward to the trip to Scotland for years. They both had Scots ancestry though their names were now the only trace of it. That's how they'd got together. She'd introduced herself as Miss McSporran on a work thing and, as often happened, a few people doubted such a name existed.

"Come off it, Ailsa. Next you'll be saying you have a twin brother called Craig."

"He's not my twin, but as it happens …"

Donald had laughed good naturedly with the rest over the failure of parents to consider the trauma they might be storing up for their children.

"I think that might possibly be even worse than preceding Duncan-MacTavish with Donald," he'd said.

"It is. I'd happily swap McSporran for your surname."

He'd faked huge surprise. "If I'd known tonight was going to be my engagement party I'd have ironed a shirt!"

A year later they got engaged for real. Neither of them were wearing crease free clothing on that occasion either. There were just too many interesting things to do and fascinating places to visit to be worried about such unimportant little details. Somehow, although they'd discussed it many times, they'd never gone to Scotland.

Until Ailsa's diagnosis it had been a vague 'we must go there sometime' idea but through the months of chemo it became a concrete plan. Something to think about and look forward to during the darker moments. There had been plenty of those but Donald had been wonderful, helping her through it all and cheering her up. He'd not been annoyingly jolly and made light of everything, but if something had been genuinely funny such as the trouble her Chinese doctor had pronouncing her surname, yet could rattle off thirteen syllable drug names with ease, he'd pointed it out.

"Who says he's saying it right anyway? He's probably just giving you aspirin and calling it cyclophospham-whatsit."

"I wish it was aspirin, then it wouldn't make me feel so bad."

"I'm glad it's not, as it wouldn't be doing you so much good."

Donald didn't shy away from the truth. She was grateful for that. They played 'platitude bingo' awarding themselves points each time someone assured her it would all be fine when that had been far from certain, or had remarked it was 'wonderful what can be done these days'. It enabled her to smile through the well-meaning concern of friends and family.

"I'm just going to sit in the car and be driven around," she'd reassured those same people when they'd asked her if she was strong enough for the trip to Scotland. In fact by then she was physically fairly well again, but had fallen into the habit of reassuring, rather than explaining, when those close to her expressed their worries.

She did sit still too, at least for most of the drive up. They'd broken their journey at a pretty cottage offering bed and breakfast in the Lake District and had gone for a stroll before dinner. They'd not lingered long the next morning though as they were both eager to cross the border.

As the sign welcoming them to Scotland came into view, Donald had reached out and taken her hand, not releasing it until they'd passed from one country into the other. "We've made it at last."

"I'm so glad to be here." She didn't think it was just the trip they were talking about.

Scotland didn't live up to her expectations; it surpassed them in every respect. The views and scenery made every photo they took look like a postcard. The air smelled so fresh and clear she was sure it must be aiding her recovery, and the people were so friendly and helpful it felt like coming home. Even the weather was on their side. Sunshine warmed them enough to be comfortable, but not so much that scrambling up hills and over rocks became hot work. The touch of autumn chill in the evenings made their hotel rooms seem extra cosy. The huge number of castles open to visitors gave them more than enough to explore and helped build good appetites for the delicious home-cooked meals of local produce.

Donald had spent the many hours, when her treatment had left her good for nothing, in researching the best places to stay and the things she'd be most interested to see. Time after time she was delighted with his choices. She'd loved the ruined castle in Threave which had to be reached by boat, and the Mull of Galloway lighthouse with its 115 steps to be climbed. She did it slowly with a couple of brief stops on the way, but she got there and earned a certificate for doing so. She'd been charmed with her first sight of Ailsa Craig and had immediately taken a picture which she'd emailed to her brother so he could share the moment.

That night they'd sat out drinking coffee laced with local whisky and watched as the tiny island disappeared into the night sky. Perhaps it was the way it seemed about to vanish which made Ailsa say, "It looks like a perfect breast."

"Not yours. They never looked like that."

"Oi cheeky!"

"Yours were always much rounder." He gestured with his hands and gave a silly leer making her giggle.

Then she told him her concerns over reconstruction surgery. "What I've got left isn't pretty, but… whatever replaced it, or covered it, we'd both know it wasn't real."

"They mentioned skin grafts and using fatty tissue from elsewhere on your body."

"Don't. It sounds like building Frankenstein with spare parts."

"Oh, Ailsa," he pulled her into a hug. "I hadn't realised it upset you so much. That you felt like this."

"I don't really, well not all the time. It's just… Well, I can see why they do the reconstructions at the same time as the lumpectomy when they can."

"You don't have to have it, love. The doctors made it clear that it's up to you."

"And you. I really want to know what you think. It would help me decide."

"At first I wanted it. I thought it would make everything back to normal, symbolise all that was behind us and I'd kind of taken it for granted it was just part of the process, not a separate decision."

"And now?"

"To be honest, even though looking at you now no one would ever know you'd been ill, I realise we can't just pretend it never happened. And I don't particularly want to see you go back into hospital if you don't need to."

As she'd predicted, his words did help. They'd reduced one of the problems weighing on her mind to a manageable decision. It had seemed all important, but really what was the big deal over how one of her breasts looked?

'Mull of Kintyre' was the song they'd chosen to have played as they'd signed the register after their wedding, so obviously it was somewhere they had to visit. The journey there was quite long, with many twists and turns and setbacks as Donald put the car into reverse and edged into a passing place to let tractors and motorhomes by. When they had lunch looking at the wonderful view and listening to Paul McCartney's song they knew it had been well worth it. Again it wasn't just the narrow road they were thinking of.

Ailsa was glad it was she who'd got sick. She had hated it all, but watching Donald go through something similar would have been so much worse. She'd known of course that it hadn't been easy for him, but she was only just beginning to understand how much he must have suffered. In a way he was still suffering because of her changed attitude to her body and reluctance to share it with him. He'd been so patient, such a good friend. Was that enough for him? For her? Ailsa resolved not to hide her body from him so much.

That night he'd not recoiled in horror when she undressed in the bedroom instead of taking a nightie into the bathroom and changing there. She'd slept naked, as she'd always done before the surgery. In the morning she'd not wriggled away as he'd pulled her close. Instead she wrapped her arms round him and kissed him. It was clear he'd have welcomed more but she still wasn't ready. Not yet.

"What's the plan today?" she asked him once she was washed and dressed.

"You know that little island that we're not sure how to pronounce?"

"We do! It's Geiger."

"Gigger!"

"Geiger, Geiger, Geiger!"

"If you'll admit it's Gigger we can get the little ferry over. There's a bronze age burial site and some of those standing stones you like and gardens and a community run hotel who do a nice line in afternoon tea apparently."

"That's cheating, but those ferries are so sweet, so let's go to Gigger."

Over a full Scots breakfast (except for the white sausage which surely nobody really ate) they learned the correct pronunciation of Gigha is much more like 'gear' than either of their versions.

After a short crossing over a sea as smoothly reflective as polished marble they studied the huge map of the island.

"That way for Achamore Gardens, the burial site and the Stone of Ogham, that way for the other standing stones."

A quick look at the scale and calculation, using their ferry tickets to measure with, showed them that attempting to see it all would involve more walking than they wanted for one day.

"The Stone of Ogham gets my vote," Ailsa said.

"Mine too."

During the walk, as well as making frequent stops to take photographs, they talked about ancient mystical places.

"They must have really believed in something to have hauled huge rocks about by hand. It wasn't just something one person did on a whim," Donald said.

"What I like best is that although we see these places must have been important we have no real idea what any of them are for."

"It's odd isn't it? I don't suppose the lives of people living on remote islands have really changed all that much in thousands of years. They still have the same landscape and weather to deal with and the same need for shelter and food."

"And for less mundane things," Ailsa suggested.

"Hmm. Whatever or whoever they got together for, the gatherings would probably have provided companionship and entertainment of a sort."

"I was thinking of druids and magic."

"You would be!" Donald said.

"So where is this magical stone anyway? The map showed it as close to the gardens and we passed them a good twenty minutes ago."

"It also showed it as being twice the size of the ferry. Either the map isn't to scale or the stone will be impossible to miss."

"Missing one stone amongst all these wouldn't be difficult, but this path looks well trodden so I guess we're on the route to something worth seeing."

They followed the track almost down to the sea on the opposite side of the island from where they'd started. Soon they were in a pretty but rocky cove.

"I was right, this is worth seeing."

"The path continues that way," Donald said. He helped Ailsa scramble over the rocks to a patch of grass edging the curved beach below.

"Lovely soft sand here, you wouldn't expect that, would you?"

"No, nor for everyone who came here to walk straight across it. Oh!"

"Sheep!" they said together as they realised they'd been following a track made by the animals which roamed the island.

"Well the sheep here are a clever lot and recognise a nice beach when they see one. This is lovely." Ailsa lay back on the short grass and wild flowers. "So warm too. I thought it would be breezy over this side."

"Fancy a swim?"

She hadn't brought a costume with her, but didn't point that out. She used to skinny dip when they were younger. He always told her they were alone and he'd keep look out. One time she'd just got out and wrapped herself in a towel when two men, carrying binoculars and cameras, appeared. They spoke reassuringly of the interesting bird life they'd just seen. Too reassuringly and Donald and Ailsa had giggled over the entries they'd put in their notebooks that afternoon.

"I'm too old for skinny dipping." It wasn't just the years and the scars left by the cancer which bothered her, but the extra pounds and stretch marks too. "Oh!"

"What?"

"I just caught myself thinking about cancer as being on equal terms with stretch marks. There really must be something special about this place."

"Then you definitely should swim. I confess I wasn't as lost as I made out. I knew this beach was here and thought it would appeal. I brought your swimsuit."

Donald took a towel and bikini from his backpack. Goodness knows where he'd dug that up from as she'd not worn one in years, but even more incredible was the fact that he'd seen her body this morning and still thought it was a good idea for her to wear a bikini.

"Someone might see."

"No, we're alone."

"Sure?"

"Absolutely." Donald grinned as though he remembered that exact conversation the day they'd met the bird watchers. He confirmed it by saying he'd keep a proper look out this time.

She believed him, even so she knew he'd be watching her too. He was still that boy who'd dared her to go in, who had been everything to her. Could she be that girl again? The one with a passion for life? She owed it to him to try.

Ailsa pulled off her sandals and took a few steps. The water was really cold. Really, really cold. She told him so.

"Wimp!"

"You won't be saying that when my skin turns blue." She tugged off her clothes and put on the bikini. It sagged where her left breast used to be, but as she sagged where her trim waist used to be she couldn't blame it for that.

The water seemed even colder when she went back and she had to paddle a long way until it was deep enough for her to swim. She couldn't take many strokes in any direction before her legs or arms touched the soft, sandy bottom but it didn't mater. She was swimming and it felt just as it used to. Almost anyway. In other places where she'd swum it felt warmer once she was in the water. Here it seemed she'd not exaggerated about her skin turning blue.

Ailsa did feel warmer once she was striding out and the sun shone onto her skin.

Donald paddled toward her with the towel. "OK, I admit you're no wimp. This water really is freezing."

She reached for the towel. "Is someone coming?"

"No. I just couldn't wait to do this." He kissed her, not like an old friend, but like the young lovers they once were.

As she dried off she knew he was still watching her. She felt his gaze stay on her as she stretched out in the sun wearing only the ill-fitting bikini.

He kissed her again. "How about it? We're still all alone …" They'd made love in the open before, way back then. That had been at the top of a hill though with good visibility of the path in both directions and that time they really were sure they were alone.

"I don't think so. Those bird watchers must be in their nineties now, we might give them a heart attack."

"Oh well, you can't blame a guy for trying."

Ailsa got dressed and they began to retrace their steps.

"I was thinking, I might see if I can get a special swimsuit – like my bras which would fit properly."

"That's a good idea."

They choose a different route back once they found footpath signs, in the hope of finding the stone. Although unsuccessful in that, they were more than compensated by the views of both Gigha island and across to Jura.

"Fantastic, isn't it?" Ailsa asked.

"It is. And if we were over there," he pointed to the mainland, "We'd see Arran, I think. There's so much to explore, we'll have to come back to Scotland."

"It's a deal."

He was right, there was much more of this beautiful country left to see. And thanks to the surgery and chemo she'd endured she had time left to do so. A country to explore and a life to live. There didn't seem a moment to lose.

"Come on," she said as she pulled Donald to his feet and then dragged him toward the ferry.

"Have you lost something?"

"No, I've found it." It was back, her passion for life, for him.

"What's your hurry then?"

"Quicker we get on that ferry the quicker we get back to our hotel room. We can lock the door and know for sure that we're all alone."

15. A Hallowe'en Curse

"Ooops, sorry," I'd said, as I collided with the back of a pointy-hatted witch at the hallowe'en party.

"Watch it, Mister, or I'll put a spell on you," she'd joked as she spun round to face me. "Oh. Hi, George."

I smiled. I couldn't speak, not when I realised who it was. I felt my face go red and my skin start to burn. I didn't need a curse; I was already under her spell."What's up? Cat got your tongue?" She opened the mouth of the toy cat on her shoulder and out popped what appeared to be a human tongue. Charlotte laughed. She looks even prettier when she laughs. "I've been hoping I'd get a chance to use that line," she told me.

I grinned; it felt good to have made her happy.

"So what have you come as?" she asked.

"A decomposing body," I just about managed to croak.

"Ooooh, sexy."

She had a point; it wasn't the most attractive of looks.

To be honest, I hadn't really wanted to go to the party which was run by the work's social club. I'd not been with the company long and was still struggling to get to grips with the job. I'd had a bit of a cold, but I didn't want to appear rude and unsociable. I can be shy and that sometimes gives the wrong impression. I'd finally agreed to go when I learnt that Charlotte would be there – without a date. There hadn't been time to come up with a decent costume, so I'd improvised one with some old bandages, fake blood and a joke finger I just happened to have.

"My magic powers aren't quite up to making drinks appear out of thin air," she said.

I can spot a hint, if it's obvious enough, and offered to fetch her one. When I returned, I was pleasantly surprised to see she was waiting for me. I'd half expected her to have used my absence to vanish.

The party was great fun from then on. Charlotte didn't declare undying love for me or anything like that, but we both agreed to join a couple of the others on a visit to the pictures, the following week. The best bit, or so I thought at the time, happened when I was about to leave. She caught hold of my arm, placed a hand on my shoulder and whispered in my ear.

"Here's the spell I promised you," she said. Then she kissed me! "That's to make sure you don't forget me."

It wasn't until the following morning I realised it wasn't a love spell but a curse. On my shoulder, right where she'd touched me, was a red oval patch. It felt a bit hot. I tried to tell myself it was just coincidence. Charming work colleagues can't really put curses on you, even if they have got you bewitched – can they?

I'd almost convinced myself the red patch was nothing to worry about, when, five days later, a rash began to develop, and spread. Small pink ovals appeared on my legs, upper arms and back. They itched.

I looked up pictures of meningitis, chickenpox and measles rashes on the internet and was sure I didn't have any of them. An allergic reaction seemed the most likely; assuming it wasn't a result of witchcraft. My cold was still with me, but I didn't feel any worse than you'd expect; just a runny nose and a sore throat, so I went to work as normal. I didn't want to take time off, not whilst I was still on my trial period. Luckily, the rash didn't show once I was dressed.

On the morning of the day I had planned to go to the pictures with Charlotte, the rash was much worse. It had spread over my chest, up my neck and down each arm. I rang the doctor's surgery, luckily they had a cancellation for that morning. Then I rang work.

Charlotte answered. "You're not just saying this to avoid going out with me, are you?" she asked after I'd explained I'd be late in.

She sounded sorry I was ill, not pleased. Of course she hadn't cursed me; that was a silly idea.

I tried not to scratch as I waited in the doctor's surgery, but that didn't stop people staring at my red blotches. I showed the rash to my doctor and explained how it had started as one patch and then spread.

"You've got pityriasis rosea," she told me. "The rash, which is thought to be caused by a virus, may continue to develop for another week or so and could cover most of your body. It should begin to fade after a few weeks and will almost certainly have gone entirely in three months' time."

"Three months?"

"Don't worry; it's just a mild rash, nothing to worry about."

"Nothing to worry about?" I almost shouted. "It itches like crazy, I look horrendous and I'll probably lose my job."

"It does look rather alarming, and I'm sorry there is nothing I can do about that, but there are things which will help with the itching. Why are you concerned about your job?"

"I've just started. If I take three months off, they'll not want to keep me on, will they?"

The doctor told me there was no need to stay away from work. "The condition isn't contagious and other than the itching, you shouldn't feel at all unwell."

"So, what's the treatment?"

"You may not need anything at all. If the itch is very troublesome, I can prescribe a steroid cream, but many people find calamine lotion or aloe vera gel are very soothing."

"OK, I'll try them." Once I knew the rash wasn't quite as bad as it looked, I felt a bit better. "What causes it?" I asked, fairly confident 'witchcraft' wasn't going to be her answer.

"There isn't always an obvious cause, but the stress over your new job may have triggered it. Some people have suffered an illness before it develops and that perhaps makes them more vulnerable."

Instead of going home, I went back to work. My boss was pleased I'd decided not to take time off. "You were right to get it looked at and check it wasn't contagious, lad. Glad you're back though, I've got a job for you and it's urgent."

I grinned. The boss realised he'd miss me if I'd taken time off. I wondered if Charlotte was missing me. At lunchtime, I went round to see.

"I can make this evening, as long as you don't mind being seen with a chap who looks like he forgot to remove his Hallowe'en costume."

She laughed, until I rolled up my sleeve.

"What on earth is that?"

"Pityriasis rosea. Don't worry, it's not catching and it's only temporary."

We did go to the pictures that night. On the way home, I told Charlotte how the rash had started and that I'd half believed she really had put a spell on me.

"Perhaps I did." She giggled.

"In that case you can jolly well come round at the weekend and put on some lotion for me – it doesn't half itch, you know."

To my surprise, she agreed.

That was three months ago. The patches have now almost faded and have stopped itching. Don't tell Charlotte though. She still comes round to rub me with lotion at the weekends and that's absolute magic.

16. Bingo, Beethoven, Burmese And Boils

I first got worried about my mate Lynne the second time she didn't want to come to bingo with me. The first time she said she was doing something else. Fair enough, I thought. To tell the truth I was pleased. Lynne doesn't get out much unless she goes with me; she's shy you see. I keep on at her to join the social club. I thought she'd taken my advice.

Don't get me wrong; I'm happy to spend time with her. She's been my best mate since we met thirty-seven years ago. In that time, I've got married, had three kids and a job in a bookies. Lynne is a spinster. She's got eight cats and gives private piano lessons. Her passions are Beethoven, Burmese and bingo, but she doesn't share them with anyone but me. Of course there are pupils at her lessons and a whole crowd of us at the social club bingo nights, but somehow Lynne still seems to keep pretty much to herself.

"Just try the social. Trust me, once you've been brave once, it'll be easy," I tell her.

"I'm not brave," she always answers.

"Lynne, for goodness sake, I'm not asking you to walk down the High Street with no knickers on. All I'm suggesting is that you walk in and say 'hello'"

She did compromise and agree to come to the bingo with me. As I'd guessed, she loved it. Still she wouldn't take the plunge and go on her own and I couldn't spend more than the odd evening away from my family.

As I say, it wasn't until the second time she said no when I called and suggested bingo that I got worried.

"I don't feel like it, Shirley," she said.

Lynne not feel like bingo? That was a first. She didn't sound well either.

"Are you ill?"

"No, I'm fine. I just don't feel like coming to bingo."

I wasn't convinced.

"How about lunch tomorrow? Where shall we meet?"

Wednesdays are market day and we'd got in the habit of meeting in town for lunch after I'd searched for bargains and she'd finished with her morning pupil.

"I think I'll give that a miss, too."

"What's up, Lynne?"

"Nothing. I told you, I'm fine," she snapped.

"Suit yourself then." I hung up wondering what I'd done to upset her. It's true that I've been pushing her to get involved in a few activities and things, but I've been doing that for ages.

A couple of days later, my youngest son told me she'd cancelled his piano lessons.

"She seemed a bit strange the last time I went and now she's cancelled the rest of my lessons and didn't say when they'd start again. I hope there's nothing serious wrong with her?"

"So do I. You said she was acting strange?"

"She didn't sit down for the whole hour and she snapped at me. That's not like her."

It wasn't. I went round to see her. She didn't seem pleased to see me and tried to fob me off.

"I've been having a lie-in and I'm not dressed."

"Don't worry about it," I said and pushed my way in. I had to push because she was trying to stand in my way. She was wearing a dressing gown, something under that, thick socks and slippers. Even when she's not dressed, Lynne wears more clothes than most people put on to go out.

"Aren't you going to offer me a cup of tea?"

She made two teas and took them into the living room. I sat on the sofa. Lynne stood looking out the window.

"So, what's wrong?" I asked her.

"Nothing."

"It's not nothing. You're not going out and you've cancelled your lessons."

It suddenly occurred to me that it might be a problem with the cats. I did a swift head count and they all seemed to be there.

"Cats OK?"

"Oh yes, they're fine. Platinum's hair is growing back really well and …"

"But you're not fine, Lynne. Come and sit down and tell me what's wrong."

"I can't."

"Of course you can. We've never had any secrets. You can tell me anything, you know that."

She took a deep breath. "I can't sit down." She turned brightest red.

"Oh dear. Have you got piles?"

I didn't think she could get any redder, but I was wrong.

"No."

"But you have got something wrong with your bum?"

She just about managed to nod, but didn't look at me.

"What is it? A boil?"

She half shrugged and dropped her head lower.

"How long has it been like it?"

"Two weeks or so."

"Since before you didn't want to go to bingo?"

She nodded again.

"That's over three weeks. I don't suppose you've been to see the doctor?"

"He's a man!"

"Flipping heck, Lynne! You won't have got anything he hasn't seen before and whatever is wrong obviously isn't going to go away on its own. You can't stand up for the rest of your life."

I did think of offering to take a look myself, but I wasn't sure she'd let me or that it'd help even if she did.

"What you need is a doctor. If you can't face seeing a man, then ask to see doctor Bell, she's nice."

"I don't know if I could do that."

Sometimes her shyness drives me mad. She'll never stand up for herself – except now she literally had no choice. That gave me an idea.

"Where's your phone book?"

I rang the health centre and explained that Lynne wanted to see a lady doctor as soon as possible. When I explained she was in pain and had been suffering for three weeks I was told that she could come down and wait and that the doctor would see her after surgery.

"Come on, get dressed. If you can't sit in the car while I drive you down, we'll need to start walking straight away."

"Oh, Shirley …" Lynne started to cry.

I put my arm round her shoulder. "It's OK, really. I'll come in with you and explain to the doctor, then you'll go behind the curtain thing and get undressed and …"

"I'm scared. When I washed this morning, there was a sticky mess …"

"And you still didn't call the doctor? I know you're shy, but letting that ruin your health is just plain daft. Go on, get dressed. If underwear will make you sore, you'll just have to go without."

"Shirley!"

"No one will know."

I didn't know if she put on any knickers or not, but she did get dressed in a loose skirt and we walked down to the health centre. I gave her a bit of a talking to on the way. Mostly so that she didn't have a chance to tell me she wasn't going in. She was pretty quiet by the time we got there. Luckily we didn't have to wait long.

"What can I do for you?" Dr Bell asked.

Lynne looked at me.

"Lynne's got a sore bu… bottom, doctor," I explained. "She was too embarrassed to tell anyone, but she hasn't been able to sit down for weeks and it's getting worse."

"I'd better take a look, then." She pulled a curtain around the bed. "Lynne, I'd like you to remove enough clothing for me to see the sore place and lie down so I can take a look. Can do that?"

Lynne stood up.

"Do you want me to go?" I asked.

"Please stay," Lynne said. "If that's all right, Doctor?"

"Whatever would make you most comfortable," Dr Bell said.

I sat and waited one side off the curtain as Lynne got undressed on the other. Dr Bell asked her if she had been feeling ill.

"No, not at all."

"Any other symptoms? For example have you been tired or thirsty?"

"No, Doctor. Well, since it became painful I have had difficulty getting to sleep."

"OK. Are you ready?"

"Yes, Doctor."

Dr Bell went behind the curtain.

"Yes, that does look sore," she said after a moment. "Did this start off as a small hard lump?"

"Yes."

"It was an abscess and it's now burst. I'll just give this a clean up to ensure all the puss has drained away."

I could see the doctor's feet moving about under the curtain for a minute or so.

"There, all done. You can get dressed now."

"Are they always on your, er, bottom?" I asked while we waited.

"Not always, although that is a very common location."

Lynne was soon out from behind the curtain.

"I'm going to prescribe you a course of antibiotics, just to ensure there's no infection."

"Thank you, Doctor."

"Lynne, you're going to be fine this time, but this must have been extremely painful and have been bothering you for quite some time."

Lynne nodded.

"If you ever have any medical issues in future, you must make an appointment, even if it does seem embarrassing."

"What exactly was wrong?" Lynne asked.

I was surprised; asking for information like that seemed almost pushy for her.

"An abscess is the formation of pus. In your case it was a boil, most likely formed by a hair root becoming infected. Usually this would be treated by a very minor procedure to drain the pus, and then a course of antibiotics. As you now know, if that isn't done, the boil gets larger and more painful until it eventually bursts."

"I know. I've been rather silly, haven't I?"

"Well, luckily it's nothing too serious this time." Dr Bell printed out a prescription and handed it to Lynne.

"Thank you, Doctor."

"I feel so stupid," Lynne said as we walked to the chemist to get her antibiotics.

"Don't be daft. Anybody could get a boil on their bum; it's nothing to get upset about."

"Exactly."

"Eh?"

"It was nothing to be upset about, yet I've risked my health and more important, I've risked our friendship."

"You haven't."

"I've avoided you and been rude. I was unpleasant to your son ..."

"You were in pain. I understand now and so will he."

"As I said to the doctor, I've been silly getting embarrassed. I've always been too shy for my own good."

I didn't argue.

Three days later, I got a call from Lynne. "Would you mind if we met for lunch on a different day in future?"

"No, that'd be OK. Why?"

"I decided to take your advice and join the social club. You were right; they're nice people and were very friendly. Starting next week, I'll be playing the piano at the tea dances every Wednesday."

"That's brilliant, but what… How …?"

"How did I get the nerve?"

"Yes."

"You were right. I discovered that once I'd done one brave thing, the rest was easy."

"Good."

"That's not all I discovered."

"Oh?"

"It's breezy walking down the High Street with no knickers on!"

17. Learning To Live In Lockdown

"Come on then, Joyce. Tell us what it is you're going to do," a colleague said.

"Yes, come on, Joyce. If you don't tell us we'll make up something shocking and tell everyone!"

I laughed at that. The lady who'd said it was so very unlikely to spread rumours that I knew she was giving me the opportunity to make up a silly story if I wanted to keep my plans secret. Doing that is something of a habit of mine. Making things up I mean, not keeping secrets. I've really only had one of those.

"I'm writing a book," I said.

Every little face on my computer screen registered surprise and several people started talking all at once. Gosh, if I'd written a sentence like that just a few years ago you'd have thought I'd started the book already and that it was science fiction! But no, this was real life. The new normal.

My works leaving do was held, very appropriately, on Zoom. It wasn't any kind of surprise as, during the pandemic, pretty much my whole life was on one kind of computer meeting or another and several aspects had continued in that way. I kept in touch with friends and family by social media messenger and chat functions. There were some phone calls, letters and cards, and actual meetings, but most communication was online. I even bought my groceries that way and had them delivered.

Work, of course, was done from home. It was all very convenient in a lot of ways. I did like being able to take my lunch break in the garden during that long sunny spell we had, and to take my daily walk whenever I wanted rather than wait until I got home at six – but I missed being with people. One person more than others I admit, but people in general too.

When my leaving date was decided we didn't know what restrictions would still be in place, so decided against a physical party.

"I'm sorry, Joyce," my boss Paul said.

"It's fine, really," I assured him. And I meant it. Saying goodbye to a my colleagues without the buffet and farewell hugs was a small disappointment compared to what some people had been through. Perhaps it was for the best. Those kinds of things can be emotional and I didn't want to make a fool of myself. And as I say, it was very appropriate. You see the remote idea, almost two years ago, that something like this could happen was sort of the reason I was leaving at all.

I'm not claiming second sight or great scientific knowledge. I didn't know back then what was coming, but as the virus spread it became clear everything would change. By the time the prime minister announced back in March 2020 that we would go into a three week lockdown, I wasn't surprised. The accounting company I worked for had begun to prepare for the possibility and as Paul's personal assistant I'd been tasked with gathering everyone's emails and mobile phone numbers, discovering what computer they had at home and issuing laptops to those few who would need them to keep in touch. We were ahead of many people in that respect.

"It occurred to me quite a while ago that a lot of our work could be done from home," Paul had explained. "And I think many staff would prefer that."

I knew they would. Some had mentioned it to me, no doubt hoping I'd try to talk him round, but he'd always insisted on face to face meetings whenever possible. I was glad about that.

Through the pandemic we kept working. There were also regular coffee break meetings at eleven each day where we could chat about non work things. It wasn't compulsory to attend these but Paul and I always did. They were the highlight of my day – those and my online work meetings with Paul. I'd been working for him for over eleven years and only then fully realised that I was in love with him. By the time we knew that first lockdown was going to be longer than three weeks I'd also realised it was hopeless. I'd started working there just after getting divorced from a man I probably should never have married. I think that's partly why I didn't realise how I felt about Paul – I'd convinced myself I didn't want another relationship. Definitely not one with a married man, as he had been when we met.

Paul got divorced a few years back. For them it was a gradual drifting apart, nothing dramatic. Nothing to scare him off future relationships, so if he'd been interested he'd have said or done something to give me a hint by now. It would have been easy as we sometimes saw each other outside work. We attended several social events together – anything where going alone would have felt awkward. Family weddings and parties. The theatre, meals out once a month or so.

Mr Johnson's lockdown announcement wasn't the shock to me that it was to many, but it had a huge impact on my life. The thought of not seeing Paul for weeks showed me how I felt about him. He'd sort of become my whole life. If I bought clothes or had my hair done I was trying to look nice for him. I took my days off to coincide with his, using the excuse that with him away there was little for me to do. It was pretty much true, but really there just seemed no point going in without him being there.

I realised I had to do something, or one day one of us would leave the company and I'd be left with no kind of life. We were both in our late fifties so although retirement wasn't a very long way off I was young enough to get another job, create a life for myself which didn't rely on one man for my happiness. I applied for early retirement and was accepted. When the pandemic hit I was asked to stay on for a year, to help them through that and make recruiting my replacement easier. I thought that a gradual break from Paul might be easier on me, so agreed.

It was during that first lockdown I decided I'd write a book. As with many people it's something I've always fancied trying. My pension wouldn't be enough to live on, but not far off. I decided I'd work part time and leave myself several days a week for the book. But what would I write? I loved reading mysteries and historical fiction, but did I know enough about police methods or any historical period? I doubted it and just occasionally I'd read a detail in a book which didn't ring true – and it spoiled the story for me. I didn't want to do that to my readers.

"What's it going to be about, Joyce?" one of my colleagues asked, echoing the thoughts I'd had myself and bringing my mind back to my online leaving party.

"Will it be fiction?" another asked.

Before I could reply the entire zoom group were asking questions, including more than one wondering if they would be in it. I explained some of the ideas I'd had.

"I haven't been able to attend writing classes, due to the lockdown, but I've read loads of advice. Write what you know came up a lot, so I thought of a dystopian story about the virus, or something similar."

"Is that what you're going to do?" someone asked, a little doubtfully.

"That doesn't seem quite your kind of thing," Paul added.

"I don't think so either," I agreed. "The reality was quite enough for me." I felt my colleagues' reactions proved I was right.

I'd started baking while in lockdown, so cookbooks had crossed my mind. When I showed everyone the cake I'd made myself, they remembered the treats I'd sent on their birthdays and said I should do that.

"I daren't. I'd have to make each recipe many times to perfect it and then I'd eat it. I've only just lost the weight I put on when the baking bug bit." I stood to give them all, but especially Paul, a twirl to reveal my still trim figure.

"Write a diet book," I was advised.

"No, I want to write a story," I said.

"Pity about the cookbook. I was hoping we could be your tasters," was said by several people in different ways. They had been. Paul had suggested, at the start of lockdown, that to help keep the team together we had little online parties for people's birthdays, just as we would have round their desk when we were in the office. When it was allowed, I'd baked a cake and he'd collected it from me, paid for the ingredients and delivered it to the person – all socially distanced obviously.

I'd had other help with the tasting. My neighbours. Louise is a single mother of three little ones, one of whom has medical issues. For years I've helped out in a small way, doing a bit of shopping for her, minding the other two when she took Alice for hospital appointments. Sometimes I went round and cooked them all a meal while Louise soaked in the bath. She never once complained, but I could see that sometimes she needed a few minutes to herself, a tiny break from her responsibilities. It seemed natural that we form a support bubble, so the four of them tasted all my bakes, and young Bill and Suzie 'helped' with stirring and decorating. It was fun, but I was glad my role wasn't full time.

I used to make up stories with the children and did consider writing a children's book. But soon realised that what was holding their attention wasn't my disjointed narrative, but the funny voices I did and encouraged them to mimic. I couldn't get that kind of thing down on a page.

The children helped with keeping my weight down too. When it was allowed I took them to the park, sometimes wheeling Alice, sometimes leaving her with her mum as I pushed the other two on the swings, encouraged them to climb over the frames and raced round whirling the roundabout ever faster. Other times I took the three of them on long walks. One day we met Paul.

From that day forward I came across him quite frequently, as we both walked in that same area at that same time several times a week. Soon we stopped pretending it was accidental and met for walks by arrangement.

"It's so good to see you, Joyce. Online meetings are fine, but I've missed you. I've felt kind of lost of late."

So had I, but not for quite the same reason. I thought it best to continue keeping that one secret. "We were a great team, Paul, but you'll get another assistant when things go back to normal."

"They won't though, will they? It will be a new normal."

"I suppose you're right." I knew the company was encouraging everyone to continue working from home as much as possible. They were moving to smaller offices so it would save them money as well as benefit staff who'd only have the commute once or twice a month.

"Besides, I don't want that. I don't want a normal you're not part of," Paul continued.

"I had no idea you felt that way," I said. How could I not have known when it's what I'd longed for?

"Neither did I," he said. "Not until it became clear the lockdown would go on and on and I'd rarely see you. When you applied for early retirement I did the same. Without you there I didn't want to continue, although I did agree to stay on and oversee the move to the new place."

What a pair we were! Both caring about each other, yet keeping it such a secret we barely knew ourselves. We were alike in many ways. I hoped that meant we'd have matching futures. One shared future.

"So, you're retiring early. And then do what? Write a book?"

He laughed. "Maybe. I hadn't really thought. How is yours going?"

I confessed that it wasn't. "I've only just decided what to write." When I told him my plan he'd offered to help with the research, and I'd very gladly accepted. It's pretty much all I've been thinking about lately, but once again my former colleagues dragged my attention back to the online party and their gentle demands to know what I was writing.

"Come on then, Joyce, tell us!"

"And quickly. This meeting will be timed out and end any moment."

I'd been counting on that, and at the very last second I said, "A love story. That's what I'm working on."

18. Quit Before It's Too Late

I come in from school and head to my room.

"Jack, I want a word with you," Mum calls as I'm halfway up the stairs.

"I'll be there in a minute, Mum," I reply.

I wonder what she wants now. Maybe I've got time for a quick drag before I get my ears bent. Now where did I hide my cigarettes?

"Now, Jack."

She doesn't sound happy, but then she's often not happy with me. Always having a go or nagging about something. 'Do your homework', 'eat your veg' or 'brush your teeth.' Never stops she doesn't; treats me like a kid all the time. I'm not a kid. Next year I'll be old enough to join the Marines, well old enough to apply. They don't let you join until you've left school. She'll stop treating me like a kid then.

"Jack, are you coming down?"

Damn, I can't find the fags. I'd better go and see what she wants, then I can have a quiet smoke in peace.

Mum holds up my ciggies as I saunter into the kitchen. She reads from the pack.

"'Smoking kills,' now why do you suppose it says that?"

"To scare people?" I guess.

"But it doesn't scare you?"

"Nah, why would it?"

"So, you think it's good for you?"

"Good for my image, gotta look tough if you're going to be a Royal Marine."

"I imagine it takes more than the right look. Others things will be important, such as good health?"

She has a point. "Loads of people smoke and are fine, look at Granddad."

"That's supposed to cheer me up? You know your Granddad is ill?"

"Fuss over nothing he said, anyway he's old."

"Jack!"

"I didn't mean he's ready to die, you know I don't want that. I just meant it's not surprising that he's not healthy at his age."

"He's sixty-nine."

"Exactly."

Granddad's a great old bloke, or used to be, but like I said, he's old. He can hardly say five words now without that awful wheezing starting up. Still, he's been smoking for years without any trouble. I hardly smoke any; I can't afford enough to do me any harm, so I don't know what the fuss is about.

"Can I have them back now, Mum?" I ask pretty reasonably.

"No you can't," she yells back and crumbles my fags up.

"Hey, they were expensive."

"You will not smoke in my house and you won't be getting any more pocket money until I'm sure you won't waste it on cigarettes."

"That's not fair."

"Oh grow up, Jack."

We don't really talk for a few days. That gives me time to wonder why she's so against smoking. Normally I can get round her all right, but not this time. Maybe it's because of Granddad. It's a shame he's not feeling too clever. He used to tell me loads of stories about being in the Royal Marines. He used to carry me on his back, pretending I was his rucksack and we'd go yomping. He taught me some self defence stuff and survival training. All kinds of stuff. He doesn't show off his medals, except for Remembrance Day. He lets me help clean them then. I want to make him proud when I join up.

"Jack, can we talk?" Mum asks eventually.

"What about?" I try not to sound too bolshy as I come back into the kitchen.

"I've been thinking about what you said, about your image, joining the military all that sort of thing. Perhaps you're right that I don't understand and I am too protective of you. You know it's just because I want the best for you, though, don't you?"

"Yeah."

She looks like she might cry or kiss me or something.

"Fancy a cup of tea?" I ask and start filling the kettle. I'm not great at all the soppy stuff.

"Maybe you should stay with your granddad for a while, he's a lot cooler than I am," Mum says.

"Granddad?" I mean, sure he was something in his day, but not now.

"He must be, he understands about the marines, he could help with your training and he wouldn't give you a hard time about smoking as he does it himself. I know he's not young, but we all get older, even you."

Mum looks sad and tired. She's always done her best for me and I know she hates it when we fall out. So do I.

"Sure Mum, I'll go to Granddad's for a while if you think it's a good idea."

She's all smiles now. "He'll be pleased."

'Course, I should have thought, this isn't about me. Mum keeps telling me that not everything is. You'd think I'd have grasped that by now. Obviously, she's worried about Gramps and wants me to look after him for a bit. I can do that, then she'll see I'm responsible.

Living with Granddad isn't like being at home. It's more like being on exercise. Everything we eat is out of tins. We keep ourselves clean and the house tidy, but there's no polishing or arranging bunches of flowers. Granddad's as wheezy as ever and he keeps gobbing up loads of phlegm. The bins soon fill up with his disgusting tissues. I miss being at home.

He shows me some old photos, him in his Royal Marines uniform complete with Green Beret, some in ceremonial gear, some in camouflage clothing. With each one I get the full story, sometimes it all sounds a bit far fetched, until he comes across a whole bundle of medal presentation pictures.

There seems no end to the things he's done and the stories he has to tell. Lots of photographs aren't formal portraits, they're snaps of him and his mates. In every one Gramps is smoking a roll up. Nearly always, the men are in uniform, often with their berets tucked into a belt loop and a smear of cam cream across their faces. They look so cool; I'm going to be just like that when I join.

"Proper hero you were," I tell him, but he doesn't think so.

"Just doing my job, lad."

"But you were brave."

"Not really. You get the training and when you're there," he gestures at the photos, "you just do what you have to."

"Do you ever see any of the others?"

"Yes, Jack and so will you; we're off to the pub tonight."

This is more like it, instead of being at home doing my homework with Mum, I'm down the pub with Granddad's ex-service mates. He's obviously told them about me. I get introduced to everyone.

"This is Road Runner, we call him that because he runs marathons."

"What about you, Jack, ever considered trying it?" the ex Marine Sergeant asks me.

"No, I couldn't do that."

"Thought you wanted to join The Corps, you can't become a Royal Marine if you're not fit."

Good point. "I'll start training and become as fit as you."

"I'd like to think you'd be a damn sight fitter than a chap of sixty-nine."

"Sixty-nine." I can't help repeating it like an idiot. This man is the same age as my Granddad but nowhere near as old, if you know what I mean.

It's great being treated like a grown up for a change. I have to drink coke of course, but that's the only difference. They don't look guilty if they swear, or keep the jokes clean for my benefit. No one says a word whenever I go outside with Granddad and a couple of the others for a smoke. Well, no one except Road Runner. He tells me Gramps is a fool to waste his cash on tobacco. He gets a pen and writes figures on a beer mat.

"What's a packet cost, at least a tenner now I bet?"

It's a fair bit more, but I agree.

"I bet the silly old duffer smokes the whole lot in a day?"

"More than one," I tell him.

"Two then, that's a hundred and forty quid a week."

Actually, Gramps often starts on a third, but I keep quiet. I'm beginning to see why he buys tinned soup and baked beans rather than steaks and takeaways.

"So, say there's fifty weeks in a year, just to make the maths easy, comes out at seven grand."

Hmm, maybe there are some advantages to not smoking.

Walking home is a slow business. Granddad's wheezing is worse than ever and he seems tired. I talk about Road Runner.

"What's his secret do you think?" I ask.

"No secret, he looks after himself that's all. Didn't you notice the difference between us?"

I don't know what he means, sure Road Runner was fitter, but he was doing the same as Gramps. They even drank the same brand of beer.

I'm still thinking about Road Runner the following morning. Granddad points him out in one of the medal presentations. I don't know if he got as many as Gramps and I'm not going to ask, but he's certainly something to live up to.

"There's still one of my ex Marine buddies that I'm in touch with, who you haven't met. He got more medals 'n me and Road Runner put together. I thought we could visit him today."

It's hard to believe the shrivelled body under the oxygen mask was once a hero. He's got something called Chronic Obstructive Pulmonary Disease. It doesn't sound or look pleasant. The bloke seems pleased we're there. Gramps chatters away to him, I can't understand half the whispered responses. Granddad's friend is soon tired and we get up to leave.

A man in a white coat is coming in as we go out. He stops to talk to us.

"So have you quit smoking yet?" he asks gramps.

"I've cut down a bit, but it's not easy, Doc."

Granddad sounds so weak, why doesn't he stand up to this bloke?

The doctor turns to me, "Perhaps you'll talk some sense into him. If you don't want your Grandfather to end up like that chap in there, then get him to quit smoking."

I don't want to think that the doctor could be right. Granddad looks upset and I can't think of anything to say. We just go.

"I can't give up lad, I'm too weak," Granddad says when we stop outside so he can get his breath back.

"You're not weak."

"Yes I am, I know what the fags do, but I can't give them up. The addiction is stronger than I am. I know it's made me ill, but I don't want you to end up like him." He pointed to the ward where his dying friend lay. "Or like me, I want you to be another Road Runner."

"Gramps, you know what you said about your medals? How it wasn't just you who won them? That you were stronger together?"

"I do. It's true. The camaraderie and support help you achieve things you'd think were impossible."

"Do you think that together we could learn to be stronger than a packet of fags?"

He looks at me for a long time. "Maybe."

We don't go straight back to his house. We stop at the health centre on the way and make an appointment for the 'stop smoking' clinic. Gramps and I will make each other proud. Mum'll be happy too.

19. Streamlining Santa

There once was a time, very many years ago,
when Santa was quite skinny – I promise that it's so.

And not just dear Santa, the helpful elves were too.
Time went by. Their little bellies grew.

Mrs Claus worried, about her husband's weight.
She knew she had to help, before it was too late.

Or Santa's bursting trousers, would show his hairy bum,
and his jacket buttons, wouldn't reach across his tum!

"You could go running, dearest. Or cycle all around."
"Oh no," said Santa. "Of that I do not like the sound."

"Oh dear," wailed Mrs Claus. "And I don't suppose,
you want to do star jumps and touching your big toes?"

Santa said he didn't, and the elves joined in his cries,
when Mrs Claus declared, "You all must exercise."

They used to work as hard, as running a marathon,
but now the toys and games, are bought from Amazon.

Although she's pleased they needn't work so hard,
Mrs Claus doesn't like to see them carry extra lard.

"If you don't swim or jump, or learn a sport to play,
you'll all be too heavy, to ride upon the sleigh.

And then you understand, all the little girls and boys,
won't get their stockings, filled with Christmas toys."

All the helpful elves opened wide their eyes,
and Santa looked very, very surprised.

"Are you trying to say my dear, you think I'm getting fat?
It's not true you know. I still fit in my hat!"

Mrs Claus was decided. Santa would have to diet.
It was a drastic action, but he really had to try it.

How she would persuade him, she had no good idea,
as unlike you and me, Santa eats but once a year.

Have you guessed, that day is Christmas Eve,
and the food he eats, is everything we leave?

If that doesn't seem so bad, I'll give as an example,
Just how much yummy grub, last year he did sample.

He ate 1,000 stilton wedges. Drank oceans of sweet sherry.
Scoffed lots of iced mince pies, made by Mary Berry.

Lemon meringue, rhubarb flan and gammon ham,
slices of lamb, strawberry jam, deep fried yam,

banana splits, trifle with custard and pouring cream.
Even something unidentifiable and alarmingly green.

Pistachios, cheese straws, marshmallows, bottled beer.
Bet you think he was full, but he was nowhere near.

The elves munched mints, licorice and things on sticks.
Santa ate a forest's worth of Twiglets – and some biscuits.

A whole chocolate log and strawberries and jelly,
sausages and sandwiches and crisps, all went in his belly.

In fact if you've ever put it out upon a plate,
Then it's certainly something that dear Santa ate.

So, I think you can very clearly see,
sorting out Santa's weight is down to you and me.

We must leave healthy food, for Santa and the elves;
Water, carrot sticks and celery. They can help themselves.

(If you fancy a quick snack, try these crudités,
and scrunch your way, to a healthy 5 a day.)

You might be thinking, this all seems rather mean,
but for Santa to be healthy, he also must be lean.

So please boys and girls, do Mrs Claus a favour,
and leave out nothing fattening, for Santa to savour.

Or Santa's bursting trouser's will show off his hairy bum,
and his jacket buttons, won't reach across his tum.

Even more importantly, you can show him what to do!
If you're really healthy, maybe Santa can be too.

So race around the garden, build castles in the sand.
Go on swings and roundabouts. Do a handstand.

Go outside and play, in the rain or sun,
and let Santa see, that exercise is fun!

And if we're really lucky, then come Christmas Day,
Santa won't be too heavy to ride upon the sleigh.

20. Her First Time

"It's easy, Fiona," her workmate, Lisa, assured her.

"Really?"

"Yes. You just lie back and think of England!" Sue said. They'd both laughed at that and Fiona had done her best to produce a convincing giggle of her own.

Fiona was nervous but she didn't want her friends to know that and have them tease her all the more. She supposed everyone was a bit apprehensive their first time. Her friends were older, they'd both done it several times by now so no longer shared her worries.

As she sat in the canteen with her mates, Fiona realised this was a chance to show her maturity. This was something adults did. Afterwards she would no longer be the child they thought her. She had worried it might hurt, but been told it didn't, not really. You just had to make sure you got someone who was experienced and had a good technique. It might be a bit painful if you ended up with some kid who fumbled about and didn't really know what he was doing, but they would advise her. Sue had already been doing it for years, and would make sure she got a real expert.

"OK, then. I'll do it," she told them.

"You sure, Fi? We don't want to force you into it if you're not ready," Sue said.

"Yes, I'm sure," she said as confidently as she could. "I have been thinking about it for quite a while now."

"You mean we've been nagging you for a while!" Lisa said.

"Well, yes that's true, but it's not just that."

"You can do it this Saturday then. Here." Sue handed Fiona a slip of paper.

Fiona rang the number her friend had given her. The friendly voice reassured her.

"Saturday at nine-thirty then."

When she made her way to the social club as he'd suggested, she hardly felt nervous at all. She was slightly early, but welcomed warmly. There was no hurry over the preliminaries. A great deal of interest was shown in her. Her lifestyle was discussed, her health, even holidays she'd been on. It was clear that every precaution for her safety and comfort would be taken. She felt relaxed as she was lead across to the bed. Her hand was taken, her arm stroked. Kind brown eyes smiled at her.

"Your first time?"

"Yes," Fiona admitted.

"Don't worry. I'll be gentle and you'll feel great afterwards."

A little blood stained the white cotton when it was over, but what she'd been told was true. It hadn't really hurt and she did feel different; happy and sure she'd done the right thing.

"Just lie there for as long as you like," she was told. "If you'd like something to eat and drink. A cup of tea and a custard cream ...?"

She smiled in response. It was good to be appreciated. Fiona was surprised more people didn't give blood.

21. Eye Eye

Darren couldn't believe what he was seeing; the woman of his dreams had just walked past him. He rubbed his eyes and looked again. She was still there. He blinked a couple of times. She was walking away from him, but he was sure it was the young woman he'd dreamt about last night.

"What's up with you?" his colleague, Tim, asked. "Seen a ghost or something?"

"What?" Darren asked then realised he'd walked out into the corridor and was staring, mouth open, after the woman. "Did you see her?"

"Who?"

"The redhead who just went by."

"Melissa?"

"You know her?"

"Well, not 'know' exactly, but I met her on Monday. Oh, I forgot you were away weren't you? She's the new occupational health whatsit."

Darren turned to look at his friend. "Tim, I dreamt about her last night."

"Dreaming? Really? You don't look as though you've slept for a week."

"Well, I have," Darren snapped.

Tim chuckled. "Melissa is the woman of your dreams is she? Well you'd better get yourself sorted out, the way you look at the moment, you'll give the poor girl nightmares."

"Thanks, Tim. You're a great mate you are." Darren was well aware he didn't look like the man of anyone's dreams.

"Just being honest. What is up with your eyes anyway?" Tim asked as they returned to their office.

"I don't know. It's not exactly my eyes, I can see OK, but the eyelids are really sore. I've had it before; it flares up from time to time. Usually I find that if I press a warm flannel on them for a few minutes, it eases the irritation, but that hasn't helped much this time."

"So what has your doctor said?"

"Nothing. I haven't been. I hate going. First you've got to persuade the receptionist to book you an appointment. You know what they're like."

"Yeah, always asking if it's medically urgent, as though we'd be ringing the doctor to lay our carpets or something."

"Exactly. Then you have to take time off work and sometimes when you get there, whatever it is has cleared up, or if it hasn't they say you should have come in sooner!" Darren shook his head, remembering his last visit to the doctor.

"I know. You can't win," Tim agreed. "Hey, I know, why don't you go and see Melissa? She's got medical training hasn't she? And it'd be a good way of getting to know her."

"No way, Tim. You just said I look like the living dead."

"I didn't say that exactly, but now you come to mention it …"

Over the next few days, Darren's eyes didn't improve. In fact, the more he thought about his problem, the worse they felt. He guessed that rubbing his eyelids wasn't helping, but they were so sore it was impossible not to.

Whenever he caught sight of Melissa, he'd go into a nearby office, or turn his back to make sure she didn't see his distinctly unattractive eyes.

At the weekend, he woke up with his eyelids stuck together and after he'd washed away the sticky discharge, he saw he'd developed a sty. He rang his doctor's surgery on Monday morning.

"Is this medically urgent?" he was asked.

"I don't know," Darren said. It seemed urgent to him, but would the doctor see it that way?

"I can make you an appointment for next Wednesday, at eleven."

"OK, thanks," Darren said.

He wore dark glasses to work. When he saw the e-mail from Melissa, he was glad he had. It stated that as the new occupational health adviser, she would be talking to each member of staff individually. Darren knew that, he'd had an e-mail last week inviting him to pop in for a chat with her. He hadn't realised she'd book appointments for those who didn't arrange their own. His was at one.

"I can't possibly go," he said to Tim.

"You'll have to, mate. Don't worry; I shouldn't think anything medical will put her off."

Darren took off the glasses. His eyelids had developed crusts, the sty was red and angry, small dandruff like flakes decorated his lids and they were inflamed and greasy.

"Yuck!" Tim said.

The phone rang. Darren answered. "Darren White, how can I help?"

"This is Melissa Black; I'm just calling to confirm your appointment for this afternoon."

"Ah, right."

"You do know where my office is?"

Darren did. He'd found out so that he could avoid it.

"Good, then I look forward to meeting you."

"Yes, me too." He heard her laugh before he hung up.

At one precisely, Darren knocked on her door and was invited in.

"Thank you for coming, I didn't think you would," Melissa greeted him.

"Why would you think that?"

"You don't like me much, do you, Darren?"

"That's not true!"

"Then why have you been avoiding me?"

It was a good question. Darren knew there was only one way he could convince her it wasn't because he disliked her. He removed his dark glasses.

"Blepharitis!" she said.

"There's no need to be like that; I can't help it."

She laughed. "Sorry, I wasn't being rude. I think that you've got a medical condition called Blepharitis."

"Oh."

Melissa came closer and gazed into his eyes. It was almost like his dream, except now she was medically, not romantically interested. "Are your eyelids sore?"

"Very."

"Have you had this before?"

"It flares up from time to time, but it's never been this bad."

"I'm sure it is Blepharitis, but you should see your doctor to be certain."

"Is there anything I can do to cure it?"

"Yes and no. It tends to recur, so you probably can't be sure to get rid of it, but there's a lot you can do to ease the problem and reduce occurrences. As it's quite bad now, I expect your doctor will prescribe you some antibiotic cream. That will help."

"I've got an appointment for next week."

"Good. In the meantime, try pressing a hot flannel on your lids for five minutes every morning and evening."

"I've done that before. You're right it does help a bit."

"Washing your eyes with a weak solution of bicarbonate of soda can help.

"OK. Anything else?"

"Don't rub them, that'll make them worse."

"I know," Darren agreed.

That night, he followed Melissa's advice.

The following day there was an e-mail from Melissa asking him how his eyes were and if he'd like to pop in at twelve. As that was lunchtime, he guessed the interest might not be purely professional. He was right.

After gazing again into his eyes, she said, "If you like, I could pop in to your office each day?" She blushed. "Er, just to see how you're getting on."

Darren's doctor confirmed the diagnosis Melissa had made the previous week.

"You've got Blepharitis. I'll prescribe some antibiotic cream. That should clear it up for now, but it's likely to recur. You'll need to keep your eyelids scrupulously clean all the time to aid treatment. That will also go some way to prevent further outbreaks."

Darren's eyelids gradually improved and, as promised, Melissa popped in almost every lunchtime to check on his progress and chat to him and Tim.

One day, when Tim was absent, she said, "You have probably guessed that my interest isn't entirely professional?"

Darren blushed. "Well, I did wonder."

"The thing is, I rather like your friend Tim."

"Oh, I see."

"I hope this isn't too cheeky, but as we're now such good friends, I wondered if you and Tim would make up a foursome with me and Tanya."

"Tanya?"

"Blonde girl in accounts?"

"Oh, yes. I know who you mean. OK, I'll ask Tim and see what he says."

That night, Darren had a lovely dream about Tanya from accounts gazing adoringly into his eyes.

22. Why Go Through All This?

The speed dating event at work had seemed quite a good idea when Jemma's colleague, Ralf, suggested they include it in the team-building activities they were co-ordinating.

"Five minutes conversation with colleagues they don't see much of will help people get to know each other," he'd said.

"True, and hopefully they'll find it fun."

"There's also the possibility of romance for some."

The last bit hadn't appealed to Jemma at the time. She'd since seen another flaw in the plan. As all single employees were encouraged to take part, Jemma as one of the organisers, couldn't get out of it.

One 'date' was Bert. The shininess of his head alone didn't bother Jemma. At thirty-two she realised her next boyfriend might not have a full head of hair. A receding hairline would have been OK, whether or not he'd shaved off the rest. Baldness due to a medical condition wouldn't have automatically earned him a cross in the 'match' column of her speed dating card either. A combover certainly would have, but in Bert's case what ruled him out for future dates was being more than twice her age. She knew because she'd sorted out his pension and was organising his leaving do.

"What's a nice and, if you don't mind me saying, very pretty girl like you doing at something like this?"

Jemma didn't mind Bert saying she was pretty. She couldn't really blame him for asking the question she'd been asking herself most of the afternoon and repeatedly during the previous six minute date.

It was supposed to be five, but George had needed time to pack away the photos of his train set. Poor man had clearly realised his chances of finding a woman willing to go back to his place, so she could climb into the loft and admire the attention to detail of his double O gauge at a ratio of one to 76, were slim.

"I vowed never to date a man from work," Jemma told Bert.

"Right… " Had he just rolled his eyes at her?

"Oh, I know it works well for lots of people, which is why I agreed to all this." She gestured around the staff canteen. "I thought it had worked for me, but he turned out to be the kind of slimeball who …" Jemma decided to confide in Bert. He was a nice man she'd probably not see again after next week. Also, other than George with his trains, she'd listened to two fairly interesting monologues from men seated opposite her and spent five minutes with a man who, on discovering she worked in HR spent two minutes telling her he'd be good at that as he had an amazing ability to get on with people and three minutes explaining how to use the online system for booking leave.

"It's really very simple once you give it a try," he assured her. He didn't give her the chance to say she already knew as she not only used it to book her own holidays but had in fact created it.

That experience had made Jemma unusually eager to say something about herself for a change.

"My horrible ex thought it was OK to take very unflattering photos of me in a bikini without my knowledge or consent. Then decided it would be funny to send me a copy saying he hoped I was sticking to salad for lunch and he was stupid enough to do it on a work computer and somehow managed to send to all."

"Oh."

"Quite. He did get in trouble for it, but I was the one who felt she had no choice but to leave. I handed in my notice and decided not to make the same mistake here."

"That still doesn't explain," he gestured around the canteen. "All this."

"When I felt ready to date again, I went on a speed dating thing in a local pub. On my way in I bumped into Ralf." He was the reason she'd begun to wonder if her promise to never date a colleague again should have had a time limit shorter than until the end of time, which she'd declared in the heat of humiliation. "I said how embarrassing it was before I realised he was there for the same reason as me, which was extra embarrassing. Then he said, 'It would be if one of us put a tick and the other a cross,' and obviously he was right."

"So you both agreed to put a cross?" Bert guessed.

"A tick actually."

"This isn't making sense, Jemma love. If it worked out between you, then you're not single and shouldn't be involved in," he waved his hand, "all this?"

"Ralf and I didn't date."

"Despite you both putting a tick against each other's name indicating your interest?"

"I told him about my no dates with colleagues rule."

"And what did Ralf say to that?"

"He told me that meeting through work is successful for a lot of people and we got on to talking about the law of averages and how many single people work here, but probably don't meet. We agreed to set up," she moved her hand, indicating the canteen, "all this."

"And if Ralf is one of the men lucky enough to sit opposite you after me, will you put a tick by his name?"

"Yes, Bert, I will."

"Good luck," Bert said as the bell rang and he got up to move on.

Jemma noticed his next mini date was with Glad who did the coffees for meetings. She was hopeful of a good outcome there.

Her own next date was with Phil, the newest employee. So new she could remember that he wore his school uniform to his interview. He had a full head of hair, and a face so smooth she was sure he hadn't started shaving. He blushed furiously as he said hello.

"Relax," Jemma said. "You got through the interview, you can get through this."

"I've said stupid things so far, or not said anything at all."

"You've got me and Glad to practise on before you get to three much younger ladies. Imagine what you'd say if you weren't shy, and try that on us."

"Um …"

"Bert said I'm very pretty," Jemma prompted.

"Did he? Um, I mean… I think you're pretty."

"Why thank you!" She kindly overlooked the fact that Phil had missed out the 'very'. "You have lovely hair," she told him.

"Thanks. I grew it myself. See, I say stupid things."

"No, humour is good. Let's try… you have nice eyes."

"So do you, but mine are luckier because they get to look at you."

"That was brilliant! Well done, Phil." They spent another couple of minutes flirting outrageously and then the bell rang. There was a long wait, because George had dropped his train photos, before everyone moved on, but eventually Phil was replaced by Justin.

"I thought you were getting married?" Jemma said.

"So did I, but Trevor and I had a huge row."

"Oh no. I'm sorry to hear that. What happened?"

"He sent a photo of us and a poem into a magazine. It was a really cheesy competition. I was so humiliated. He won a couple of tacky T-shirts with our photo and the poem on, can you imagine?"

Jemma, looking at the very smartly dressed Justin, said, "I can't imagine you wearing it, no. Nor can I imagine why you're upset that the man you love, publicly declared his love for you and did so with such eloquence he won a prize. That's not humiliating, but I'll tell you what is." She described her own experience with a photo being made public without her prior knowledge.

"Oh my! You poor thing. Trevor would never do anything half so awful."

"Then he sounds like a keeper."

"He is. As soon as," he made an extravagant sweeping gesture with his arm, "all this is over, I'll call him and beg his forgiveness."

"Good luck."

The man after Justin told her that he and another participant had got on so well that nice as Jemma seemed it didn't feel right to try to chat her up.

"Good attitude. I really hope it works out and if it does, will you promise me you'll never photograph her without her knowledge."

"Of course I won't. That'd be creepy."

"The kind of thing only a total slimeball would do?"

"Totally. Oh crikey, that's happened to you, hasn't it?"

"Yeah," Jemma admitted.

"Run a mile! If he's thoughtless enough to do that, there's no telling what other awful stuff he'll get up to."

"You're right. He's history."

There was an even longer gap than usual before Jemma's next date arrived, because George had found someone who thought he was really clever to have created trees and buildings in the same scale as his trains and offered to use her metalworking skills to produce bridges and sidings and… When they got to that point it was suggested the two of them stay where they were for the remainder of the evening.

Jemma's next date was a young lad who pointed to George and said, "Well, doesn't that just prove there's somebody for everyone?"

"That does seem to be the case. Have you found a possible someone?"

"That your way of saying you won't be ticking my box?" he asked.

"Oh, sorry… I… "

He chuckled. "Don't worry, just teasing. I've already marked down three people I think it will be fun to get to know better. That's probably enough to be going on with."

Jemma hadn't spoken with all of the men present before the final bell went and didn't put a single tick on her card, but she wasn't disappointed. That was the advantage of not having got her hopes up beforehand.

The following day at work, three gifts arrived for Jemma.

"Yesterday was a success for you then?" Ralf asked.

"In a way. George sent me a very small metal cat, because he knows I like them and it's a little too large to sit on his train platform."

"Amazing how much you can get to know people at these sort of events. We've worked together for months and I didn't realise you have a passion for cats."

"I haven't. They're nice looking creatures but their attraction yesterday was as a slight break in the torrent of information about trains."

"Ah. The other things look more promising."

"The chocolates are from young Phil, who is going on his first ever date tonight."

"OK."

"Not with me."

"Of course not. You don't date men from work."

"I don't think Phil will count as a man for another year or two and anyway, I've updated that rule."

"You have?"

"I thought that if I was to receive a dozen proofs that it wouldn't be a disaster, I might try again."

"Right. Everyone, except George and Louise had a dozen dates last night. Were all yours undisasters, if that's a word?"

"I don't think it is, but yes, they were all positive in some way. Some were fun, one gave me a chance to look at past mistakes and several of the others convinced me I'd just been unlucky and most men aren't slimeballs. Even the mansplainer reminded me how excellent I am at my job, which includes being a good judge of people."

"That's great. So the flowers are from a man you met last night?"

"Julian. He and Trevor have made it up and the wedding is back on."

"That's good news. For them obviously, but possibly for me too?"

Jemma produced the 'match' card she'd not bothered handing in, added Ralf's name and put a big tick by it.

23. Nice And Naughty

"Happy Easter darling," Kevin said as he handed his wife a beautifully wrapped parcel. It was about the size and shape of an egg box.

Vickie gritted her teeth as she took the gift from him. It was heavy and by the feel she guessed it contained six creme eggs. Vickie had always loved creme eggs; until she'd started her diet that was. She didn't need to look them up in her calorie list to know they weren't something she should be eating. It wasn't even as though she could just break of a small piece at a time. With a creme egg any normal person has to eat the whole thing at once. Any person with willpower like Vickie's has to eat the whole pack in a very short space of time. Why couldn't Kevin understand that although he'd given her chocolate eggs every year since they were together and she'd always enjoyed them, they weren't what she now wanted? He just grinned at her and waited for her to open the present.

She couldn't manage a grateful smile, but she did refrain from any strongly worded complaints. She held the parcel still with both hands to prevent them shaking with angry frustration. She gazed down at the shiny paper and gauzy bow so that he wouldn't see her disappointed tears. She wasn't upset just because he'd given her an unwanted gift, but because he didn't seem to understand her, no matter how carefully she'd try to explain it.

She'd been slim when they met, well perhaps curvy was more accurate, but she certainly hadn't been fat. After they married, she began to put on a bit of weight.

"That's because you're contented," Kevin told her when she mentioned it. He seemed pleased to be the source of the contentment and clearly wasn't worried by a few extra pounds. Vickie became pregnant and gained more weight.

"You're blooming, love," Kevin said as he gently caressed her belly.

She had only shifted half the gained weight by the time she became pregnant a second time. Again she put on weight and failed to lose it all after the birth. By their tenth anniversary a friend joked that there was two stone of Vickie that Kevin wasn't married too. She'd been upset, but Kevin had hugged her.

"Lucky me, now there's even more of you to love."

Her weight continued to creep up. She tried not to notice, or at least not to let it worry her too much. Most of the time she'd succeeded, until a month before Christmas. They'd been invited to a party and Vickie went shopping for an outfit. After visiting every shop in the High Street, she'd been unable to find a dress to fit. She was used to having difficulty finding anything that looked good on her, but this year she couldn't even find something that would do up. She'd gone home in tears. Kevin had tried to comfort her.

"Never mind love, those High Street stores just cater for skinny young things, we'll find something on the internet."

They'd ordered a dress and gone to the party. Vickie knew she was the only one there who'd had to order her dress especially because no standard shop sold clothes large enough. The biggest woman there apart from herself was wearing a dress that was identical to one that Vickie had tried and failed to squeeze into. She was quiet throughout the party and too upset to eat anything. At home, Kevin had tried to understand.

"It's true that you're not tiny, but what does that matter? In any group of people there's always one who's the biggest."

"Yes, and it's always me," Vickie said.

"I love you just as you are, and as long as you're healthy and happy I don't see that it matters what you weigh."

Vickie agreed with him, but as she was neither happy nor healthy, it didn't help. She got breathless walking upstairs, her hair and skin looked awful and she felt so lethargic all the time. She went into the bathroom and eased out of the dress, vowing that never again would she have to order one from an outsize specialist. That was another problem, here she was undressing in the bathroom, because she was too ashamed of her body to let her loving husband see it.

"You can't really fancy me," she told Kevin.

He tried to prove her wrong, but she was too tired to respond.

Vickie knew that even if her wobbly bits didn't put him off, they were making her unhappy. She went to her doctor.

"Many of your problems could be greatly improved with a few lifestyle changes. Your poor diet and sedentary lifestyle aren't just responsible for excess weight. Your tiredness and poor complexion are one result. Do you have any other problems?"

"Not really."

"No breathlessness, pains in your joints, constipation?"

"Well, a bit yes."

"And you know your weight could be causing other serious medical problems?"

"You mean heart attacks, diabetes stuff like that?"

"Yes, but please don't get too worried. If you adopt a healthier lifestyle and lose the excess weight you'll greatly reduce the risk."

"I know doctor, but it's not easy to change my habits."

"Small changes can make a difference. Try to get some exercise every day. You don't need to join a gym, just do something that gets you slightly out of breath and keep it up for as long as possible."

Vickie giggled as she imagined explaining that one to Kevin.

"If you are thinking of sex, then yes, that can be good exercise."

Vickie grinned at him, maybe the doctor really could help her.

"Here are some leaflets on other types of exercise. Swimming is good as it doesn't put strain on your joints, but you must find something you enjoy. I'm also going to refer you to a dietician. In the meantime try to eat plenty of fruit and vegetables."

Vickie followed the advice of her doctor and the dietician; at the end of the first week she'd lost three pounds. She felt great. The next week she lost two more and was really pleased with herself. During the third week the novelty of all the salads and fruit began to wear thin.

"I really fancy some cheese cake," she told Kevin.

He went straight down the shop, saying he wanted the evening paper. He came back with a gorgeous portion of white chocolate cheesecake, "As a reward for doing so well."

She wasn't angry with him, but felt guilty about giving in to the temptation and eating the whole thing as well as her proper supper.

To avoid too much temptation at Christmas she stocked the fridge with healthy food and didn't buy the usual boxes of shortcake, bags of crisps and tins of chocolates. Instead, she bought a few of Kevin's favourite nibbles and gave the children a selection box each. She was sure that if all the 'naughty' food was someone else's she'd manage to resist eating it. Her plan almost worked.

Kevin bought her an enormous box of Belgian truffles, some liqueur chocolates, a Toblerone so large he'd needed two sheets of paper to wrap it and a novelty chocolate reindeer with jelly bean droppings. He also gave her an enormous dressing gown bought from the same supplier as her party dress. At first she'd thought he'd given her a whole set of towels and had been annoyed at receiving something to be used by the whole family as a present. She'd been really upset when she realised that this enormous mound of towelling was a single garment for herself.

Vickie tried not to show how unhappy she was with the choice of gifts, but Kevin guessed he'd got it wrong.

"Sorry love, I thought you deserved a few treats at Christmas."

"I know you were just trying to be kind, but I really do want to lose weight."

"I keep telling you, I love you how you are. You don't have to give up things you enjoy on my account."

"It's not just for you. I want to lose weight for myself too."

When Vickie explained how unhappy she was and how ill she felt, Kevin promised to help her.

"Take the chocolates into work and share them out. I'll get you another present in the sales."

Kevin bought her a pair of training shoes and the whole family began taking regular walks together. At first, Vickie tired quickly, but gradually she began to go a little further each time.

The family ate healthy meals and whenever they fancied a fattening treat, they took care to eat them out of Vickie's sight. She steadily lost weight and became healthier and happier. Kevin noticed the difference.

"You look even better than you did five years ago and I certainly can't complain about your increased energy levels," he remarked in bed one evening.

That's why Vickie was so upset at the gift Kevin had just given her. He understood that she wanted to lose weight, she was doing extremely well, but still had more to lose. He'd agreed to help and could appreciate the difference it was making, so why on earth was he giving her chocolate eggs? If he'd wanted to give her a gift why not flowers or a basket of fruit? Perhaps it was a test of her willpower. Well, she could do without that! Maybe he'd got fed up with her and this was his way of saying she might as well give up trying to be attractive as no one would want her.

Vickie took a deep breath. She tugged at the pale pink wisp of ribbon and let it fall. She undid the paper and revealed an egg box. A real one. She opened it. Inside were six kiwi fruit. She looked up at Kevin.

"I didn't want you to feel you were missing out when the kids ate their chocolate ones."

Vickie hugged her husband, then whilst the kids went to their grandparents for an egg hunt, she and Kevin burnt up a few more calories.

24. Oh, What's Called?

I switched my phone on straight after work and saw I'd missed a call from Gran. I rang straight back.

"Hello, Abigail love, how are you?" she asked.

"I'm fine, Gran. And well done for getting my name right," I teased.

"That's the beauty of these gadgets – the names show up before I answer."

She usually does get mine right, but Gran is notoriously bad with names. Apparently she had sleepless nights before her wedding, worried she'd get Granddad's wrong during her vows. It's called nominal dysphasia and she's always been like it. She's great at coping by using endearments and descriptions when she can, so people don't always notice.

It's only the names of people and things Gran gets mixed up, not the people or items themselves, and she's perfectly normal in other ways… Well, maybe normal is overdoing it, but she's as sharp and clear thinking as she ever was.

"Is there something bizarre, borderline illegal yet well intentioned, you want me to help with?" I asked.

She laughed. "Not right now. How is college?"

I'm only doing cookery evening classes, but Gran is really proud of me for having enrolled. That's despite her knowing why I did. Or maybe it's because of that.

"It's fine thanks. We did pastry this week. I'll make you a pie if you like." I was sure she would like. Although very fond of the results, and more than capable of producing them, she's not an enthusiastic baker.

"That would be lovely. Can you do that fancy one with the sliced up… the fruits?"

"Cherries? Apples? Plums?"

"Apples, and you leave the peel on and arrange them so it looks pretty."

"Ah! Tarte tatin."

"That's it, yes."

"OK, I'll get all the stuff in my lunch break tomorrow."

"How's that boyfriend of yours? What's his name?"

"Simon?" I don't have a boyfriend, but it must be him she meant. I work with Simon. We started on the same day, so did our training together and it seemed natural to make friends. I'd like to be more than that, but I'm too shy to do much about it. When I saw him looking at the college prospectus, I said I was thinking of doing a class. When he asked which one, I had to sneak a look at what was on offer in order to give an answer. To my surprise he said he'd signed up for cookery himself.

"Yes, Simon, that's right."

"He's fine, but we're just friends, Gran."

"Yes, yes. Did you get that dress I told you about?"

"I did go and try it on, but I'm not sure it's really me."

"Of course it is. It's beautiful!"

"Ye-es." It was, but it was also quite low cut, decidedly slinky and extremely vibrant.

"Never mind. I've got the answer!"

"You have?" I wasn't aware there was a question.

"I've signed us up for that thing and after that it will all work out. Don't worry, we'll do it together."

I wouldn't say I was worried precisely. Just slightly apprehensive. Gran has involved me in some of her schemes in the past. We've yarn bombed all manner of local landmarks and over three different years she's had me helping to arrange stones on the beach to spell out 'Marry me?' on Valentine's Day. She wasn't proposing to anyone, she just hoped it would persuade a few couples into getting married.

Gran is very keen on weddings. She and I were both bridesmaids at her friend Beryl's wedding last year. She asked us because one of Gran's schemes, involving bubble wrap, luminous orange paint and a lot of explaining to a thankfully amused cricket groundsman, had resulted in Beryl and George finally getting together.

"Gran, what is it we'll be doing?"

"I've forgotten the name. Something foreign."

"Feng shui?" I've no idea why I said something so unlikely.

"What's that?"

"It's where people put furniture and things in the right place for harmony and good luck, I think."

"Come on, love. You've seen my flat. There's no room to shift furniture."

That was a slight exaggeration, but I saw her point. What she didn't say, because she's usually tactful, is that if anyone wanted help moving furniture they wouldn't ask me. Sometimes I do dislodge things by knocking into them with my wheelchair, but it's always accidental.

"Is it ikebana?" That's some kind of flower arranging. I wouldn't have minded trying that.

"Never heard of it. I'll pick you up at seven next Saturday. That gives you just over a week to practise."

It would have done, had I known what I was to practise.

In a quiet moment at work I tried folding up waste paper in case Gran had booked us onto an origami workshop. Simon came to see what I was doing and had a try. We managed a paper airplane which nose dived straight to the floor, something that very vaguely resembled a fish, and to laugh so much we attracted the boss's attention. We quickly got back to work, and had everything done by home time.

I kept trying to think what Gran might have signed us up to. There weren't many clues, apart from the fact I was supposed to practise. That ruled out Kung Fu, Taekwondo and Jiu Jitsu, at least I hoped it did. Gran does tend to think I'm capable of anything. Thanks to her encouragement I've achieved things others might think were beyond a girl in a wheelchair, but I didn't imagine she'd expect me to attempt martial arts before even being shown the moves. Come to think of it Gran always says she gets plenty of exercise jumping to conclusions and running into trouble, so it really didn't sound like her sort of thing. Could it be Pilates? I wasn't sure exactly what that involved, but I'd heard it's a gentle form of exercise.

Partly in the hope of jogging her memory, I decided to tease Gran. I put on my dressing gown and tied it closed with one of dad's dark ties and took a selfie of me doing what I hoped looked like a karate chop. I sent it to Gran with the message that practise was going well. She was soon on the phone!

"What on earth are you playing at, girl?"

"I'm practising, like you told me."

"I am not taking you down the pub wearing your night clothes!"

No, she wanted me to wear that slinky dress which revealed a lot more than my cosy PJs do. Oh, the pub on Saturday night... "Karaoke! That's what we're doing, isn't it?"

"What else would it be?"

I didn't list the possibilities as it dawned on me what she'd meant by saying she had the answer. Simon had told me he was starting a band. I longed to be part of that. When I'd told Gran she said I should offer to be their lead singer. It wasn't a terrible idea as not only do I love to warble away, but I'm actually quite good. Of course the main reason I wanted to be in the band was to spend more time with Simon, but I'd enjoy the singing too. Unfortunately I was far too shy to suggest it, and opportunities to demonstrate musical ability don't come up very often in the office. I had joined in when a few people started singing 'Food Glorious Food' in our evening class, but I doubt I could be heard over the way everyone else was belting it out.

Karaoke wasn't a terrible idea of Gran's either. You might think I'd be too shy to get up on stage, but that doesn't scare me the way letting Simon know how I feel would. Besides, Gran would be with me.

I started making plans. Firstly we choose which song – 'You're The One That I Want' from Grease. Of course I didn't rely on just using the title when discussing it. Titles are like names and I've been in the library with Gran when she's been asking for a particular book. She may have requested 'The Silence of the Lambs', but that wasn't what she wanted to read!

I sang her a few lines to check we really were talking about the same song.

"That's it," Gran confirmed. "My voice is deeper so I'll be… what's his name?""

"John Travolta?"

"Yes and you can be, um, her. That poor, lovely girl."

I was glad I knew I'd be playing the part of Olivia Newton John as it would have taken a lot of wild guesses to get from Gran's description to her name.

Other than picking the song, my plans involved selecting a nice sensible outfit and telling a few colleagues that I'd be singing on Saturday. Hopefully someone would film it and show Simon, he'd ask me to join his band, then to go out with him and we'd live happily ever after. Obviously there would be a wedding with Gran as guest of honour, but I was getting ahead of myself.

I practised every chance I could get, both on my own and with Gran. There aren't any names in 'You're The One That I Want', so pretty soon we were both word perfect. We even choreographed a bit of a routine with me doing the whole shoulder shaking thing, and Gran throwing off a leather jacket and spinning me around in my wheelchair in a rough imitation of the moves from the film.

On Saturday Gran arrived early – to give me time to put on the slinky dress she'd bought for me and insisted I wear.

"That… um girl… the one in the film. She wears a slinky silk outfit," she reminded me.

"It was black and it wasn't a dress… " Although as soon as I said that and remembered the skin tight top and trousers Olivia Newton John did wear, the dress didn't seem such a bad option.

When we arrived I was amazed to see Simon in the pub. Not only that but he'd saved space for Gran and me. To be honest he probably wasn't prepared for Gran, but then very few people are.

"You must be Matthias," she said, when he returned with drinks for both of us. "I've heard a lot about you."

That was odd. Not her getting the name wrong obviously, but that she'd said something so unusual. I don't think she knows anyone of that name. There was also the confidence with which she said it. Gran is fully aware she's likely to make a mistake, so often offers names almost apologetically.

"You're not as tall as I expected," she added.

That was odd too. I didn't think I'd described Simon, not physically anyway. I'd probably said a lot about him being lovely and gentle and things like that. Simon is close to six feet, so why would Gran think him short?

"Nor as broad."

This was getting weird. Simon is nicely proportioned and Gran is usually much more tactful.

"At least you're dressed sensibly," Gran conceded.

"Um, thanks," Simon said.

"Some rich people like to show off with lots of botox watches and you phones and cowboy boots."

I thought I knew what she meant with the first two, but the cowboy boots still have me stumped. Whatever she was up to, I had to put a stop to it.

"Gran, this is Simon. My friend from work and who does the same cookery evening classes I do."

"Oh! Hello, Simon." She shook his hand enthusiastically. "I've heard about you too. If I'm honest ..."

"Gran, I think we'd better go and see about our music," I said, rather firmly.

"Yes, I suppose we'd better. You stay there and listen hard young man. My granddaughter is a wonderful singer. She should be in a band!"

"Right," Simon said. He looked uncomfortable and who can blame him?

I wheeled myself away, wondering why Gran had said what she did. It had been deliberate, I was sure. I quickly realised she was trying to make Simon think he had a tall, muscle bound, and wealthy rival. Could that possibly be why he'd not looked entirely happy? He had come to hear me sing, and in the busy pub he'd have had to make a bit of an effort to keep a table free. Maybe he was just being a good friend, but it was just possible there was more to it.

I'd put him right about that part of Gran's scheme to get us together as soon as I could. First though I needed to give a stellar performance and prove I deserved a place in his band, and his heart.

As soon as we began singing I relaxed and enjoyed myself. Gran seemed to as well, although maybe she relaxed too much as she didn't quite hit all the notes – unless she was deliberately singing slightly less well than usual so I seemed better in comparison? It was the kind of thing she might do.

When we rejoined Simon he praised our performance.

"She was good, wasn't she?" Gran said. "And don't you think she's prettier than Hugh Ferning Whittingstall?"

"Definitely," Simon agreed. "A lot prettier."

"Ask her to join your band and go out with you then."

"Gran! I don't want him pushed into asking."

"But you do want me to ask?" Simon said.

I nodded to admit as much.

"Abigail, will you please come out with me?"

What to do? As I'd said, I didn't want him pushed into asking, but now he had it might be hurtful if I refused, and I really wanted to say yes. Gran was no help as she'd vanished. Of course she had. She's usually tactful.

"Before you answer, there's something I need to tell you," Simon said. "There is no band… Well, there's me with my guitar and my little brother has a tambourine, but there's no way I'd have the nerve to play in public."

"So why did you …?"

"Sorry, Abigail, I was trying to impress you. It was a stupid thing to say."

"Yes," I said.

"I know. Thing is, I'm really shy. I pretend not to be and as a result I blurt out stupid things. I wasn't even thinking of doing an evening class, I just picked up the leaflet hoping I could start a conversation about what we did in the evenings, then when you said you were interested it seemed a good way to see more of you."

"I meant yes, I'd like to go out with you." There was a lot more I could have explained, such as the reason I was doing Karaoke, why Gran had called him Matthias and my huge relief that no band meant she wouldn't go round claiming to be related to someone in the Beatles or ABBA.

There wasn't time though as Gran was back. "Come with me, you two. I've discovered that the lady who runs the kangaroo machine is in love with the bar manager, and I've got a brilliant idea to help get them together."

Thank you for reading this book. I hope you enjoyed it. If you did, I'd really appreciate a short review on Amazon, Goodreads – or anywhere else.

I can be found at www.patsycollins.co.uk You may like to sign up for my newsletter and get a free story, plus news of the latest releases, special offers and behind the scenes insights. A link can be found on the website, or you can use subscribepage.io/ItLSNa

A Clean Bill Of Health
Your Good Health

Just A Job
Perfect Timing
A Way With Words
Dressed to Impress
Coffee & Cake
Making A Move
Days To Remember
Not A Drop To Drink
Unearthing The Truth

Non-fiction

From Story Idea To Reader
(co-written with Rosemary J. Kind)

A Year Of Ideas:
365 sets of writing prompts and exercises

Novels

Firestarter
Escape To The Country
A Year And A Day
Paint Me A Picture
Leave Nothing But Footprints
Acting Like A Killer

Little Mallow cosy mystery series

Disguised Murder and Community Spirit in Little Mallow
Dependable Friends and Deceitful Neighbours
in Little Mallow
Deadly Words and Innocent Gossip in Little Mallow

www.ingramcontent.com/pod-product-compliance
Lightning Source LLC
Chambersburg PA
CBHW070459170726
48291CB00008B/2572